Sillies, Fancies, and Trifles

SILLIES, FANCIES, AND TRIFLES

A Collection of Shorts

Peter Kostoglou

RESOURCE *Publications* · Eugene, Oregon

SILLIES, FANCIES, AND TRIFLES
A Collection of Shorts

Resource Publications
An Imprint of Wipf and Stock Publishers
199 W. 8th Ave., Suite 3
Eugene, OR 97401

www.wipfandstock.com

PAPERBACK ISBN: 979-8-3852-0769-5
HARDCOVER ISBN: 979-8-3852-0770-1
EBOOK ISBN: 979-8-3852-0771-8

VERSION NUMBER 01/22/24

DEDICATED TO MY FAMILY:

MAMA, BABA,
GREGGY, PINA,
GEORGIE AND DAVID

WITH A BOUNDLESS LOVE
AND MORE!

"Let's start a new page . . ."

"Who then is the greatest in the Kingdom of Heaven?"

Jesus called a little child . . . set him in the midst of them, and said:

"Assuredly, I say to you, unless you are converted and become as little children, you will by no means enter the Kingdom of Heaven"

—Matthew 18:1-3

A BRIEF WORD BEFORE
WE BEGIN . . .

THESE FORTHCOMING WORDS ARE not simply or merely words. They are much, much more than that. To me, they are something akin to protracted or extended spells or enchantments, perhaps magical, perhaps charming, perhaps fanciful, perhaps disarming, or perhaps a crazy combination of nothing, something, and everything in between, but nonetheless, at bottom, (I hope) captivating, bewitching, and enthralling.

When I was a young child, I used to genuinely and sincerely believe in magic. Then I grew up a little, and life began to happen to me, and I thought what a foolish thing to believe in. So, I stopped. But I continued growing, and experiencing, and becoming, and now, as someone older though still young at heart, I cannot help but feel that this "magic" is more real than anything—whether that is for better or worse.

What is this magic I speak of? As the great Hamlet declares: "words, words, words." Words that dance, words that play, words that tickle, kiss, caress, capture, hold, and envelop us. Words that eat us up and spit us back out whole, anew. Words to catch us when we fall or lift us up when we are down. Words to make us angry, to make us think, to make us act, to make us cry, to make us laugh, to make us smile. In essence, words to make us *feel* deeply and intensely what it means to be.

I read these words, I see how each letter flows and follows fantastically one after the other. I see how the 'c' curves to cater for the comet that is destined to come out of it, or how the 'h' hooks so that you might hang and hold your hat or jacket on after a long, hard day, or even how the 'w' dips and rises again corresponding with the dolphin that jumps in and out of the water *ad infinitum*. Most of all, I see how words create and transform. I feel how they worm along, how they get caught, stuck, cocoon themselves on the page, but most importantly, I feel how they transfigure and metamorphize into butterflies, how they grow wings and silhouette and pirouette across the plain of our hearts, coloring all the otherwise grey spaces in between.

I am forced to think of myself, and I cannot help but think of my own infinitesimal 'smallness,' especially against the backdrop of the vastness of the world, our world, which contains in it stars, and moons, and galaxies, and *you*! And yet paradoxically, sometimes, when I stand on the threshold of a precipice, and gaze out penetratingly into the night, when I perceive and experience all these things, I cannot help but feel indefatigably 'big'. It is as if I am somehow almost larger than life, above it, beyond it, as if somehow it is solely all *for* me.

On these occasions, when I feel and experience these hymns, lullabies, and symphonies, I call out into the distance "I am–!" and in its echo, a whole new world opens up to me, crashes, and courses through me, tears me apart and reforges me from inside out.

Fernando Pessoa once wrote, "what you see is not what you see but who you are," and I am in love with those words. I could go on quoting hundreds of such lines that attest to this grand mystery of ours, with each one another tree planted in a great apple orchid that would be able to sustain us until eternity comes, but I shall not bore you. Perhaps that is to each his own duty and responsibility, since as we all know, "an apple a day keeps the medicine man away." Alas, my point here is concerned with the magic of words; with their power to intoxicate us, their power to take us away to far distant lands, and ultimately, their power to help us brave, endure, overcome, and indeed, even redeem life—that is, to make us better, to make us more beautiful.

If that is not magic, I am afraid I would not be sure what is. The only other thing of course I could think of is Love, and perhaps the two are somehow inextricably and intimately linked. But we shall have to save that discussion for some other occasion.

With all that being said and out of the way, I now draw the curtain and open this window to the waves. Please run along the seashore of my spirit and dive deep into the ocean of my imagination. Whether the water is crystal clear, alkaline, or murky, I cannot say, but I expect it will be cool and crisp, and at times, perhaps even refreshing. Consider this your fair warning, dear reader. So, without any further ado, please enjoy and enamor yourself today, tomorrow, and maybe even the day after that, in these sillies, fancies, and trifles.

ONAWISH

*"Perhaps everything that frightens us is, in its deepest
essence, something helpless that wants our love."*

—Rainer Maria Rilke.

Everyone remembers their first birthday. Well, perhaps not
their actual first birthday per se because that is quite some distance away but their sixth or seventh or even their tenth birthday.
Or, in other words, and for our purposes, their 'first' birthday.
And this was no different for the young boy, our hero, who was
overcome by the magic and aura of Birthday on that fateful day,
as we shall come to see.

In the Arkadi household, the family had just finished dinner
that night, and the three children were carrying off the plates and
dishes to make room for what the young boy was most looking
forward to—dessert, and more specifically, his birthday cake.

He could not help but be in his mother's way as she was clean-
ing up, and so with some annoyance, yet still gently, she told him
to sit down at the head of the table, by his father's side, so that she
and his sisters could prepare his surprise in peace.

He listened obligingly, though reluctantly, and as he waited
his mouth salivated, as there was nothing he wanted nor desired
more at that instant.

1

Soon, his mother turned off the dining room lights, and his sisters emerged from the kitchen carrying together the biggest, most dazzling, and most delicious birthday cake he had ever seen, all the while his family joined in their special rendition of the usual and customary birthday song:

"Happy birthday to you
You're a hundred and two
You look like a—
And you smell like one too!"

The young boy cooed and giggled with tremendous, ecstatic delight as his sisters placed the cake in front of him. The cake's candles shone like a spotlight, reminding them all that he really was the center of the universe, if only for that evening. And as if he could not be any happier, his mother said his two most-liked and treasured words—"you're favorite"—and he beamed even brighter than the spotlight, like a full moon in the clear night sky.

Indeed, it was his favorite—a chocolate mud cake of course, lathered with layers of vanilla frosting, doused with sprinkles, and covered with a beyond generous array of candies, marshmallows, and jellybeans which were scattered haphazardly on top. After all, the young boy only celebrated that birthday once.

"Happy birthday," said his dad, with a tear and a smile, seeing before him all that his son was and all that he might become, "may you be granted whatever you wish for, so long as you say it on a wish."

"Onawish?" the young boy exclaimed curiously, "where's that?"

"No silly–" said his father, before he was silenced by that particular glare from his wife. She had always been far more delicate in dealing with such fancies and trifles so that he was all too happy to succumb and let her take over and explain.

"Onawish," the young boy's mother described gently, "is a special place where you come to be, a place between Dream and Imagination, where Eternity becomes an Eve. It is the place where

Creativity and Possibility first blossom and meet, beyond even Doubt and Fear, mingling and mixing to carve out Destiny."

The young boy looked at his mother, eyes wide with wonder. "That's all well and good, but how do I get there?" he asked innocently.

By now, his father had cottoned on, and replied with a twinkle in his eyes and smile, "*honor-wish*."

The young boy kept turning those words over in his heart and mind.

"Onawish, Onawish, Onawish. What does that even mean?"

"Enough now!" said his sisters in unison, feeling Boredom beginning to creep over them. "Blow out your candles before they melt," they insisted, though really, they just wanted to eat.

"And don't forget to make that wish," his mother quickly added.

The young boy closed his eyes and inhaled deeply, letting his longing and yearning carry him away. "Onawish," he said to himself, but quickly took that back. He could wish for anything, so he thought he should wish bigger, brighter, better. Instead, he wished to be a superhero, since he thought that if he was a superhero, he could not only visit Onawish (since, as we all know, superheroes can go anywhere) but he could also have superpowers (since, as we all know, superheroes can do anything) and therefore, he thought he could get so much more out of his wish. Such was the young boy's logic. In fact, not just any superhero did he wish to be, for he realized he could be one that he might not like. Instead, he wished precisely to be a big and strong superman, indeed, just like his father.

And on that wish, he opened his eyes and blew out his candles in one swift go, hoping that his wish would be carried away and fulfilled in that place where wishes usually go to come true, wherever that place may be.

Having done so, his dad removed the candles and began to cut a nice, big, thick slice of cake and apportion it out to each member of the family. And they all scoffed it down hungrily, all the while the young boy waited, and waited, and waited.

Seeing the young boy lost in thought, his father said to him under his breath, "don't worry my boy, wishes take time. You can't get the fruit without having done the labor."

The young boy was somewhat comforted and looked at his father expectantly. He smiled knowingly at him in return, a smile fit for his age and experience, and then said more loudly so that all could hear:

"You better eat your cake otherwise your sisters will have no trouble eating it for you."

The young boy burst out, "never!" and he devoured his cake more greedily than the rest of them combined.

And amidst all that colorful and delicious chatter, laughter, and hullabaloo, Joy found a home for the night, and their cake-smeared faces bore the marks and gifts of its coming, as if some magic really had been conjured up and brought to bear. And nothing looked so beautiful and so good as a happy family united under the roof of a happy home, even if it was just for the night.

It is here dear reader that I must give fair warning that something fantastic occurred. As if a rabbit had been pulled out of thin air, or water had been turned into wine, some concoction of words must have been connected together and uttered aloud in such a way that as the young boy jumped onto the couch that night to read a story, as he always did since that was his custom, in the space between a wink and a sniffle, the couch gave way and he fell through as effortlessly as one slips through a dream, so that he disappeared without so much as a trace.

Where he vanished to, who could say. But he was very much alive, for although he was discombobulated, he felt himself falling like at the end of those peculiar nightmares or dreams, depending on your interpretation of them.

The young boy plummeted through the air narrowly missing certain particles, which he assumed to be rocks, that glittered and flitted past him. So caught up was he that he was sure that he had been swept along and away by a meteor shower, which if true, I must record would be the first known instance of such a kind.

Whatever the case, he screamed with all his might, but his voice sounded no more than a teensy-weensy, teeny-tiny squeal, like the noise a dragonfly's wing might make when it whizzes past one's ear. And this squeal continued until the young boy landed with an outstandingly phenomenal plop, headfirst, into this cream, velvety, sponge-like heap.

The young boy dug himself out, not without quite some difficulty, dusted himself off, and collected himself all the while licking his lips clean, enjoying that foreign yet somehow familiar sweet and sticky taste left on his skin.

"Where am I?" thought he, as he gazed out and poked at the colorful, mountainous conglomerate that sprawled out and enveloped him, almost as far as his eyes could see.

His mother's words flashed through his mind as subtly as a blink. But they quickly passed. He thought not, for this was real, tangible, able to be seen, felt, lived in, breathed in, in every sense of those words, whereas he could not say the same for Onawish.

The young boy ran his finger over a green blob. He took a few more steps and then pressed it into a purple one. A hint of French vanilla mixed with frangipane wafted through the air.

"Why is this place so sticky, and why does it smell so sweet?" he muttered out loud to himself.

But he found no answer as he wandered about aimlessly.

By now, the young boy had grown tired from trudging around through this heap for so long that he sought rest. He saw a white, cloud-like blob and approached it lackadaisically, for he felt that this would make an excellent pillow. Yet as he unburdened himself, and let his weight fall on this supposed cushion, he was immediately startled, for he bounced back up as if he was on some tremendous trampoline. And despite his best efforts and adjustments to keep himself down, nothing seemed to work, for this blob happened to be preposterously buoyant.

Finally, as the young boy managed to find some respite and relief, he began to feel that there was something strangely intimate about the place, as if he had experienced it all before. This is not to suggest or say that the young boy had *actually* experienced *this* itself before, nor that he was delusional or had some other mental or psychological ailment or malady that prompted such fantasies or illusions, but rather that he had undergone and experienced such similar intimations, presentiments, and sensations that he could not help but feel that they were somehow one and the same, or at the very least, connected so deeply, albeit mysteriously, with each other.

The young boy closed his eyes. Again, he took in his surroundings, this time with new eyes. A certain zeal overcame him as he tried to figure out whether this might be his birthday surprise.

Something caught his attention. Behind him. His trail. His footprints, like in sand, had borne their imprint and left their mark. But rather than leaving the velvety-like cream where it was, his steps had instead displaced it and revealed a thick, glossy mud-like base underneath.

It could not be!

The young boy fell to his knees and began to dig. He dug wildly, frantically, manically, until he had made a hole the size of a box that he would be able to get inside and fit in.

Then the incredible happened. What possessed him, who knows? Perhaps the same thing that possesses children to attempt to run through walls, climb and jump from tall trees, fall in love, or even grow up, but whatever it was, it bewitched the young boy to take a handful of that muddy floor, bring it to his mouth, and eat it.

And eat it he did, with such immediacy, such vigor, such appreciativeness, that it would perhaps be far more accurate and astute to say that he inhaled and devoured it.

Behold! By some miracle, this mud was exquisite. And the young boy sucked each of his fingers, then hands clean with a long drawn out and delightful mmm mmm mmm.

"My birthday cake!" he exclaimed, and if you have not already guessed by now, the young boy was indeed correct. He found himself on his birthday cake. The ground was the vanilla frosting which covered the chocolate mud-cake, and the different colored blobs and globs were the candies, marshmallows, and jellybeans. Everything now made sense to him. All was perfectly natural and seemed as it should be except either he had significantly shrunk so that the birthday cake now imprisoned him, or the birthday cake had so egregiously enlarged to an almost cosmic proportion, that he was left behind.

Whatever the case he rejoiced at what he thought was his good fortune. He fell onto his back, and rolled around in pure, unadulterated pleasure, for it is not every day one finds themselves standing on their birthday cake, let alone any dessert for that matter, and enchanted in ways beyond belief.

Were you to find yourself in the same situation, what would you do?

For the young boy, an answer to this question was quick and easy. He instantly had two overwhelming desires. The first was to jump on the birthday cake as if it was a bouncing castle, assuming that the sponginess of the cake would serve as a superb spring. And so, he began to jump. However, he very quickly realized that rather than having that splendid springiness he so charmingly thought, the texture of the birthday cake was much more akin to quicksand in which he sank right through to just under his waist so that he really had to struggle to pull himself back out.

His second desire was to devour as much of his remaining birthday cake as physically possible because he thought that there soon might not be any more left if he were to leave it for another occasion (a very fair and reasonable presumption given his family, especially his two sisters, who "ate like horses" respectively, as the proverbial saying goes). So, the young boy ate, and ate, and ate until he could eat no more, and he collapsed under his own weight, burping and belching bubbles that were all the colors of the rainbow. The young boy grinned and giggled, savoring the moment and quite literally carving out its memory in Time.

And as if things could not get any better, a crisp shade began to come over him and he felt a lemon-sized droplet of wet fall on him, that not only rinsed the cake from his skin, but cooled him too. Oh, what joy, what glee he felt right about then.

But the more the young boy basked in the shade, the more it loomed, until soon, ominous it became. What had been a soft, gentle shade now became an almost pitch black, bitter, biting darkness. What was a light coolness, now became a spine-chilling freeze. And whatever prior, short-lived peacefulness the young boy thought had been, now became totally and utterly disturbed.

The ground began to rumble an earth battering, cake shattering rumble as if a volcano had erupted from deep within. What can only be described as a shiny, rotund saucepan fell towards the young boy as petrifying and menacingly as ash and debris. And the young boy stood paralyzed, stuck in the cake, about as useful as a house trying to outrun and escape the threat and terror of a lava flow.

As the shiny saucepan descended, the young boy stared at his enlarged, bobble-like head in its reflection, with a look of bewilderment and stupefaction. Right about that time when all should have been it, when all should have been over, when he should have been crushed, this enormous spoon (for that is what it really was) swooped to the side and scooped a piece of the cake, mind you, a piece that the young boy all the while stood helplessly on, and brought it back up.

He was raised towards the sky, as if being recalled especially by the hand of God to the Heavens, until before long, the young boy had come face to face with the beast—a giant! Though not just any giant was he, rather a giant that very much shared and resembled almost exactly all the features and likeness of the young boy himself.

The young boy was literally a stickybeak, so he was able to get quite a good look at this . . . this . . . Thing.

"Dad!?" he called out, after an intense while, dumbfounded and perplexed. Whether the giant could not hear him, or chose not to care, whatever it may have been, he did not respond, and worse still ignored the young boy as if he was not even there. A hot, orange-sized droplet of saliva now fell onto the slice. The giant brought the spoon to his mouth slowly, relishing and savoring each moment of marvelous anticipation.

"Dad! It's me, your son! Don't eat me!" shouted the young boy, all the while he waved his hands frantically, for what else was he to do.

But the giant continued on his way, salivating greedily as a sure sign of the delight that was soon bound and certain to come.

The young boy trembled and tried to run, but from his terror, he had sunk ever so slowly deeper and deeper into his birthday cake so that it was as if he now found himself wading through a thick cement bog.

His father drew the spoon to his mouth, licked his lips salaciously and bit. And though the young boy tried to jump off the cake with all his might, he was impossibly stuck and was slurped and swallowed up like the end of a strand of spaghetti.

Inside the giant's mouth, the young boy tossed, and turned, swirled, and whirled, rumbled, and tumbled, up-ways, down-ways, side-ways, this way, that way, and every which way, that it was nothing short of a miracle that he was not chomped into pieces, let alone survived the ordeal at all. And like a shipwrecked sailor, all the young boy could do was keep his head above the sludge and try to stay afloat.

But this was only the beginning of his trial since, as everybody knows, what is chewed must necessarily also be swallowed. Thus, the young boy was carried away in the sludge down his father's esophagus into the belly of the beast where he supposed he would meet his end, either by poison, asphyxiation, a cruel cocktail of them both, or perhaps even something far, far worse.

Now reader, I must stress that I am by no means an expert concerning human anatomy or physiology so what happens next, though undoubtedly remarkable, should most probably and in all likelihood be taken with a grain of salt.

As the young boy spilled down the esophagus like some perverse slippery slide, in his frazzled state he tried to grip and claw at the flesh until he managed to catch hold of a groove, and thereby support himself on it as if he was on a step ladder. And as the food continued to drop into the seemingly bottomless abyss, he clung onto those steps with dear life and tried to climb up the ladder to safety, if we could call it that, or otherwise anywhere else other than Here.

Through that combination of instinct, adrenaline, and fatigue, it occurred to the young boy that if his father had one spoon of cake, what was to stop him from having more. And if he did have more, which was undoubtedly likely, then it would be far worse for him to try and escape out of the same way he came in.

So instead, the young boy determined to push himself through the esophagus to see where else he could go. He forced and wedged himself through with all his might, and now found himself in a mirrored pipeline, or in today's language, what we would call the trachea. Yet being the size of an eyelash, and perhaps far more ticklish, for each part of his body could creep and crawl, he was bound to cause a cataclysmic reaction in the hyper-sensitive windpipe, the magnitude of which would be no less than discovering hundreds of thousands of spiders running all over and covering you in your sleep.

And a reaction he did cause, because suddenly the giant began to gurgle and grumble monumentally, and a great gust of air began to brew, rising out of his very depths.

The young boy could feel his father long battling to stifle it here, repress it there, stop it completely, but to no avail. For just like his love, that was the inevitability of this cough. And cough the giant did, though it was much more like a ferocious howl.

Now, to escape this great gust of air, that came up like a breath of fire from a dragon protecting its golden hoard deep within its den, the young boy used all the momentum and force he could muster up to jump through the flesh of this windpipe like a torpedo. And again, he succeeded, although not without having the soles of his socks scorched and singed.

Where of all places did the young boy end up now? The ever-beating, life-giving, mystical palace of the heart. Yet, it was in no way, shape, or form what he had expected.

The chamber was dark and shadowy, permeated by a distinct, pungent odor that could only be born out of years of weariness and neglect. Worse still, it was filled and covered with cobwebs, specters, and creepy-crawlies of Loneliness, Isolation, and Despair. An icy silence filled out the space like a thick fog, chilling the young boy to his core, only cut by the spasmodic beat of a sunken heart that pumped who knew what anymore. In all, it had become a chasm where Shame and Not-Good-Enough ruled mercilessly.

Though the young boy did not know what to do, he set about to do something, if only to do something lest he should hopelessly do nothing at all. And as he stumbled around, he clung to his father's words and pressed them close to his chest as armor for protection—"that it is in darkness we make a name for ourselves, when we brave and endure it until the coming of the light."

For a start, the young boy went about sweeping the cobwebs and sooty parts of his father's heart to open up the space, so that he might breathe easier, and some light could be allowed to seep in. So too did he go about shooing away the ghosts and phantoms that continued to linger, float about, and haunt him which he did sometimes with a kind and gentle word, and other times, with a sharp, cutting, and severe admonishment or reprimand. Whatever the case, it seemed to work for his words were heard and felt, and the apparitions fled like bats before a concentrated, searing, bright light. All this the young boy did so that the palace might become somewhat more comfortable, worthy, and befitting of its name.

And with this done, a ray of light, like a seedling of a star, peeped in, and the heart all of a sudden began to remember itself.

Now with a bit more light, the young boy could see clearer, and he soon discovered what was causing all this heart's grief. A terrifyingly large tumor had coiled itself around the aorta like an immense viper, choking, sucking, and feeding on the life from it.

The young boy walked to that spot and examined the stain intensely. The blackness continued to swell up fiercely like an oil spill in the ocean, staring wrathfully at him since he had disturbed and upset its peace and tranquility.

"My gosh dad. I didn't know you were like this," said the young boy sadly taken aback.

But the tumor did not speak. Instead, it tried jumping at the young boy, on several occasions, with almost a hiss, seeking to devour and swallow him up too.

It was clear that self-contempt and shame, like the many-headed hydra it was, had buried itself deep inside the young boy's father, tempting him so that he would fall by summoning up all his guilt. But it is only by cutting off each of its heads as they appear, that we grow, for we are what we live with, what we put up with, what we allow and focus ourselves on.

The young boy prepared himself to go to war for his father. It was only fair, proper, and right, given that his father had not only fought for him and his family, but also for anyone and everyone who was in need, for so long. He *needed* to fight for his father, just as he knew that his father would unhesitatingly and unflinchingly fight for him.

The young boy grabbed the neck of the tumor, that viper. As he touched it, he was flooded by thousands of his father's hidden and buried thoughts. He could sense and feel all his hurt and pain, his perpetual aching, his silent self-condemnation for not being present, for not being good enough, for bringing dishonor, and worst of all, for continuously falling short and letting him down. Oh, the shame and despair he felt.

The young boy was desperate to do something to help his father, so he grabbed the tumor and squeezed it as tightly as he could.

"I'm sorry dad!" he screamed painfully as it quivered and convulsed, "I have to do this, it must be done."

Now, the tumor began to transfigure, metastasize, and morph into thousands of different memories that the young boy loved, if only to repel him. He saw his first father-son breakfast at school, the time his dad taught him to ride his bike, their first pillow fort, that one particular chocolate ice cream they always had at the beach, and even the time they stayed up all night together to see if Santa was real.

"You're not sorry! You don't care."

"I do," said the young boy, "I'm doing this for you."

The young boy squeezed harder and harder, and the harder he pressed the tumor the more spiteful it became, and the more violently did the giant wither, tremble, and shake, like a single, lonesome flower in a storm.

"You hate me! You want to destroy me!"

"No dad," answered the young boy, "I only want to help you."

"Help me? Like this? And to think I would call you, my son."

A tear welled in the young boy's eye. But he shook himself free of the viper's clutches.

"Let me go!"

But the young boy refused. He only squeezed harder and harder.

"I'm doing this because *I love you!*"

With its final breath, the tumor managed to spit out venomously, "love me? You want to kill me."

And killed it is just what the young boy did, all the while repeating those three blessed words as if they were a magic spell. The tumor exploded and burst into thousands of tiny black fragments of ash and dust, which the boy collected and cleaned, and his father's heart began to beat again with vivid vigor, unburdened and free.

Having thus contended valiantly and formidably, the young boy crashed, and however long he lay there, he soon saw the steady glow and felt the tender warmth of the heart's hearth that had been rekindled and lit. An uncreated, glowing white, iridescent, and incandescent light transcended and endowed the space with the breath of new Life, and the chamber shone resplendently, in all its ineffable glory. Truly, his father's heart was now worthy of being called a palace, a home.

Is this what it meant to be big and strong, to be a superhero like his father? To hold the weight of the world in your heart if only for the sake of the ones you love? To struggle and sacrifice over and over again, each time with the great snake when it appears to you with newly shed skin? To bear the responsibility of it all and not say a word or complaint against it? And protect all those close to you so that they too might be able to flourish and become? If so, then the young boy would carry and bear that weight, despite its pain, despite its hardship, and despite its affliction. For if his father's love was so sure and steady, and knew no bounds, then neither would his.

In order to save his father, the young boy had offered himself, and he only managed to do so because of his pure and true love for him. Now, he reconciled himself to the fact that he was trapped, with no escape, in his father's heart, his new home outside and beyond 'real' life. Why? Because once there, it would take more than a lifetime for someone to release and set you free from inside their bosom. He bowed his head and prayed:

> *"I cry out from my depths,*
> *Lord, hear my voice,*
> *As you were raised, lift me up also,*
> *And let me dwell in you,*
> *By your side."*

When a prayer is said in such earnest, it cannot help but grow wings and ascend to the ear of the Great Listener, who in return, in *His* loving kindness, sends forth something like a Dove, bearing his blessing of peace and consolation.

Suddenly, his father's heart began to beat with the vivacity of the Ocean, sending out waves of gentleness and calm, so that the young boy felt himself being pulled in by the strength of its ebbtide. His father's heart now opened up to him and he could not help but unconsciously draw near.

"Help me! Save me! Have mercy on me!" said the young boy wearily, as he gave himself up exhausted, and fell into his father's heart with open arms.

And just like that, as soon as they touched, as soon as they felt each other's connection, the young boy opened his eyes and found himself being cradled in the safe haven of his father's arms on the couch, gently rocking back and forth, all the while being whispered to, soothingly.

"What happened?" the young boy asked searchingly.

His father looked at him, full of emotion, as if a whole life flashed and passed before his very eyes.

"I think you got your wish," he replied, smiling seriously, "you almost passed out from eating all that cake."

But all the young boy seemed to hear was, "Onawish." Was he a superhero? Perhaps on this occasion he may have been, perhaps he would need to do more so that he might be one on every occasion. All he knew was that if this is what it meant to be big and strong, to be like his father—to brave and endure—then so too would he choose to be, if only to be even half of his father.

That was no small realization, for the young boy now fully seemed to understand that he was being raised on the shoulders of giants.

Honour-wish. That the young boy had done, and in so doing had inaugurated a journey that would span across his lifetime, a journey that knows no limits or bounds, a journey that one day might forge him into that superman he could be. *Honour-wish,* and you might become all that you are meant and destined to be.

The young boy looked up at his father and hugged him, "I love you, dad."

His father's eyes moistened. He pulled his son in closer and hugged him tighter. "I love you more."

"Maybe so for now . . ." thought the young boy, ". . . but just you wait and see."

And the two remained embracing for some time, in what was the most natural, perfect, and ecstatic of harmonies and unions, unsure of who needed that hug more. Nevertheless, that hug seemed to say everything, especially the things both father and son considered inexpressible and left unsaid. After all, what can't a hug contain?

THE CONFERENCE
OF THE TREES

*"One does not covet the stars; he rejoins
in their splendour."*

—JOHANN WOLFGANG VON GOETHE.

OUR STORY BEGINS IN bygone days; before the days of Man,
before the days of animals, even before the days of Being itself;
before the days of lands and seas, before the days of Seasons, even
before the rhythms of Day themselves. Rather, our story begins at
the time when the Great Sower roamed the formless and shape-
less earth, alone.

As he wandered, he was numbed by an airless air, an air that
seemed to spring out of the immense abyss of Emptiness, Time-
lessness, and Spacelessness and follow him like a shroud. This air
persisted and would not let up or cease whether he walked, ran,
leaped, crouched, or even lay. Perhaps it was an air that we might
name Loneliness.

And though this air chilled him, it also kissed him, caressed
him, tickled him, inspired him, encouraged him, and even moved
him. So moved was the Great Sower that he decided to consecrate
this moment by planting a seedling in the void, if only to fill it.

The Great Sower knelt down to his right, and with tender love and care, planted a seed so that he might have a companion for himself to bask and share in his joy.

This seed he named Shema, the first of his beloved.

Very soon after, before he even had time to contemplate his work, let alone determine whether it was good, Consciousness and Thought assailed him.

"What should this seedling do when you are no longer here?"

To that the Great Sower replied that it did not matter, for he would always be here, even if only in spirit.

But that was not enough to satisfy Consciousness and Thought. Instead, they continued to contend with him.

"And what should happen, that in spite of this, the seedling becomes lonely, worse still, forgets you?"

The Great Sower, whether he foresaw and knew or not, made no answer. Instead, he thought, let me make it too a companion so that they might share in my joy together, with me too. And this is just what he did.

He knelt down on that very same spot, and again with tender love and care, planted another seedling, this time to his left.

This seed he named Iver, the next of his beloved.

The Great Sower stood back and admired his work. He smiled, for he knew that it was good. Then he declared in a voiceless voice out of which all other voices would emerge:

"Rise! Become what you are."

And the seedlings obeyed and did so. And from them, not only did Time itself start and begin to pass and flow freely, but so too did all other things begin to sprout and spring fourth, growing out of them. With this, the Great Sower rested for he knew that delicate things such as these take time before they come fully into fruition.

Days passed, and soon they turned into weeks. Weeks turned into months, and months turned into years. Seasons too passed from Summer to Autumn just as verily as Winter passes onto Spring, all the while Shema and Iver grew, and grew, and grew, exposed to, and nurtured by Nature itself.

Eventually, eons had passed, and the Great Sower awoke in the shade of two almighty trees. Such were they now, that perhaps they could have even rivalled the Tree of Life and the Tree of the Knowledge of Good and Evil themselves. He looked up and gazed at how they had risen. He was filled and moved by paternal feelings for he believed that since they had grown so much, they too had come to realize and share in his wisdom and awareness, and that their joy and love knew no bounds just like his own. He rose up to meet them and spoke:

"Shema! Iver! It is me."

Both trees felt the strength of his voice course through them and stood in awe of the power of his being. Despite how tall they had grown, somebody was not only able to converse and communicate with them, but also, and more importantly, connect with them.

"Where have you been all this time?" Iver broke in.

"And since you are of us, will you continue to be with us now?" Shema added.

The Great Sower smiled upon his seeds, his beloved children, and the trees radiated and glowed under his beam.

"I spoke to you once when you were little, just when you were born, and you listened. I have come to speak with you once more before I bid you farewell and depart."

"But why? Why are you leaving us so soon?"

"I'm not leaving you," the Great Sower replied, "I'm simply returning inside of you to where I really dwell. For we are one and the same."

Though still unsure, at these words the two trees stared at each other and were touched by the deep feelings of reverence, in that way only trees can be affected.

"Why do you look at each other like that?" asked the Great Sower pre-emptively, "have you already grown weary of each other?"

The two trees looked away sheepishly, although I could really say treeishly.

"Do not be weary, you were made for one another," said the Great Sower, "you have so much left to grow into. In fact, as far out as you see, to the horizon, all the way from East to West is yours to relish in and enjoy, so long as you choose to do so with each other."

"Why is that?" the two trees asked simultaneously.

The Great Sower smiled heartily upon them.

"That is for you to determine and discover. But now, before I go, I tell you, *be what you are called to be!*"

With those words, the Great Sower raised himself above them and melted into the sun, and his streams of light descended upon Shema and Iver like millions of shining and shimmering sparkles, causing them to ignite from inside out. And the two trees shone resplendently as if they were inflamed and ablaze.

After a while, Iver said aloud strangely, "and what must we be?"

"This!" Shema responded chastely, gesticulating.

"And what is *this*?" asked Iver sharply, as if trying to prick him with a sword since he was not content with that response.

Shema struggled thoughtfully, trying to find the right words to express himself. After a while, he answered innocently:

"Tree."

With this response, both Shema and Iver stood firmly rooted in their ground, each contemplating in their own way what that word meant. For how long they meditated, who could say, after all, what is time to the trees? But before long, they were interrupted by the music and noises of a score of happy children that had undoubtedly come out to play in their space.

Now, the two trees were in the days of Man and thus, they thought it best to ask the children for an answer to their supposed riddle.

"Children," Iver declared in a voice that unintentionally thundered, "will you tell us what is Tree?"

But perhaps either because of the height difference or language barrier between them, the children did not hear nor could they understand, and therefore, made no reply.

"Stupid children," thought Iver, "as if they would know what it is to be us anyways. We are trees, for God's sake, what could they know."

"Don't say that," said Shema gently, "perhaps they just hear differently, comprehend differently, speak differently to us. Perhaps they will show us what it means."

"How?"

"Through their emotions, then we can *really* see."

"So, what are you saying?" asked Iver, with an ever-increasing intensity.

"Rather than asking them what tree is, let us just be. Then we can decide and determine what they think about it, what they think about us."

"A wager," proclaimed Iver, "I like that."

"No not a wager, I just meant . . . " started Shema before he was quite viciously cut off.

"Enough! We shall see who the better Tree is."

And so, Shema reluctantly, and Iver proudly went about treeing as only such trees can tree.

Being Summer, the children found themselves boiling and melting so that they sought shade among the low hanging, leafy branches of the trees. On this occasion, Shema delighted in the children's presence for he was all too happy to have more company. So, he presented himself in such a way, like that of a good host, that ensured that each child would find pleasure in their welcome. They grabbed Shema's branches and began to fan one another, aided by the help of Shema himself who rustled and shook his leaves too, if only to create more of a breeze for one another so that they might be refreshed.

"How cool is this," the children joined in together, as they laughed and continued playing in what Shema deemed his safe keeping.

Meanwhile, Iver stood conceitedly, indulging himself in the sun. How vain he thought to himself as he watched on. It was precisely this heat he wanted, needed, pure, uninterrupted, unsullied heat, which if he could only soak all up, might help him to reach the stars. Then he could rightfully pronounce himself truly as Tree, or in other words, as the greatest tree among all the trees, and win his wager.

Soon after, another group of children sought refuge amidst Iver's branches, but he immediately became suspicious, thinking that they would spoil and take his heat away. Iver maneuvered himself in such a way as to conceal his branches so that he stood about as worthless and demented as an umbrella in a hailstorm. Because of this, the children found no respite or relief amidst his branches and leaves as there was neither shade nor breeze.

"That's right, leave!" Iver declared to himself victoriously, as the children departed in search of some other tree's better company. "No one shall take my light," as if they were really capable of such sorcery.

Now, whether Iver wanted himself to be heard or this particular child's ears were peculiarly attuned to the sounds of the forest, whatever the case, despite her doubts, she seemed to take notice of his words. She whispered her thoughts to the group, and this inaugurated what was to be the beginning of one big, and I mean really big, tremendous, extraordinary, cosmic game among them all.

By now, Autumn had come, and just like the trees, the children wanted to mimic life, and so they climbed up them really high if only to fall and repeat it over and over again. Those same children did not find Shema difficult to climb, not because he was an easy, simple, or undemanding tree, but rather because he arranged himself in such a way that if they could twist and turn themselves agilely and rightly, then they could mount and move along the branches as swiftly and smoothly as a logical sequence. And the children passed their time in this way, climbing, and climbing, and climbing until they were very high up in the sky.

"Wow! . . . Oh my! . . . Cool!" the children joined in together delightfully, as they admired and were breath-taken by the view. And Shema had no trouble sharing in their joy, for it was a view he knew all too well. In fact, his happiness only increased because he could share it with others who appreciated it as much as he.

All this hurrying and scurrying up and down Shema as if he were a carnival ride brought so much laughter and bliss that even if the children slipped, tripped, mis-stepped, or God forbid, even fell, they were in too much rapture to notice, let alone care, so that they never really seemed to seriously hurt themselves. Bar a few scratches here, and some splinters there, in other words, scars befitting of an original and interesting story to tell, it was as if the children had been cast under a spell, of whose magic might only have been captured in scenes befitting and worthy of Klimt.

Just as the children were enjoying their game with Shema, whether they were aware of it or not, the other children, not to be outdone, wished to partake in this same game with Iver. So, they did, or at least tried to.

The children attempted to climb onto Iver's branches but being cunning and wily, he shed himself of his bark so they could not get a good hold of the branches and instead slipped and fell. Yet the children refused to let up or slacken. They conspired together so that they might surmount him, and this in turn became the name of their game. The children gave each other piggy-backs and tried to raise themselves on each other's shoulders to reach the higher hanging branches from which they could then help the others up.

But seeing this, like a desert cactus, Iver became dry, prickly, and thorny, ensuring that any body part that tried to lay hold of him would lacerate, splinter, or cut. And the children had no choice but to let go, even if this was entirely against their wills and wishes. The children could not mount him, no matter how much or hard they tried. Instead, they were forced to leave teary-eyed, with bloody fingers and arms, and sore bones, which they perceived to be attacks against their very existence, against their very being itself.

The children rallied together, and right before they left out of sight, they turned and glared at Iver with looks that could scorch.

"We'll show you!" said the foremost one of them, as the others beat their breasts and called out in agreement.

And all Iver could do was look down haughtily upon them, laugh, and gloat, and repeat aloud, "I dare you! Prove it! We shall see!"

And he continued carrying on as that self-same proud and almighty tree that he took himself to be. But of course, the children neither heard nor saw this because of the vast chasm and differences in their being.

All the children left, and only returned to the two trees in the Wintertime, for each season brought with it new opportunities, mysteries and most of all, moments for play. It was this the children looked forward to most. Why? Because if the trees were there to help them in the Summer, then they hoped they would not abandon and forsake them now that they needed their help in the Winter. If the trees had once cooled them, then now, they hoped they might warm them too. This they evinced for themselves to be the ultimate harmonious partnership and union between them both.

So, the same children set about lopping and chopping branches so that they might have enough firewood to see them through the snowy season. After everything Shema had given them, the children tried to go about this unhappy but necessary work as gently, reverently, and caringly as they could, aware that this would undoubtedly deeply affect the tree. This seemed to be confirmed because as they cut the tree, they thought they could feel and hear its wounded sighs and whimpers. And as painful as it must have been for him, Shema gave all of himself to them freely and they were left in abundance, even though the children had sought his wood only scarcely and sparingly. They respected one another enough to know when to be fruitful with each other and when to yield, and as a result of this, they were blessed a thousand times over.

Is this what it meant to be?

Whereas Shema gave himself voluntarily to the children, Iver smugly and stubbornly refused. He was Tree, and he thought he was the most supreme and superior of them too. If this was so, he thought to himself, why should he let a handful of people, worse still, a handful of pathetic, little children desecrate, degrade, and defile him for their enjoyment and pleasure? To allow or permit this would be blasphemous, sacrilege, contrary to everything that he thought it meant to be Tree.

The children attempted to break Iver's branches for firewood but to no avail. Soon, they realized they would need saws, axes, and chainsaws to aid them. When they returned, they set about their work carefully, but soon began to thrash and bash at the tree because they could not make any headway otherwise. For every scratch they were able to inflict on Iver, he returned to them chipped saws, ever-blunting axes, and wrecked chainsaws until they could not work with their tools anymore. Iver's skin was almost as impenetrable as corrugated iron, and the children left without so much as even some woodchips.

Finally, the children gave up and cursed aloud:

"This is no tree", they kept proclaiming, "it is something wicked, something malevolent, something . . . far, far worse."

As they departed, Iver sprinkled on them some tree chippings and bark, gloatingly, as a testament of his superiority over, and benevolence towards them. What could they tell him about being a tree he thought, as the children walked away covered in dust, despair, and defeat.

"Was that really worth all your energy?" Shema asked, once the children had long gone so that they were all alone.

"What?"

"That . . ." answered Shema trying to express himself as simply, clearly, and accurately as he could, "to go against your . . . nature?"

"What nature is that?" Iver spat, "I am Tree. Unlike you I shall not be made to be subservient to Man."

"I'm not that though, either."

"Really? Look at you," said Iver contemptuously, "you're a shell of yourself, not even half the tree you could be. Look at how different, alien, unlike you are compared to me."

"Everything passes you know, however, that doesn't mean it is the end."

"That's just it. I won't! I refuse! I refuse to pass, to end, and I will do everything to remain here," said Iver ferociously.

"And at what cost shall that be?"

"Just you wait and see."

The two trees stood in solemn, somber silence for the rest of that Winter, meditating and deep in thought. Before they had even began to address and try to alleviate their melancholy, it seemed to have moved on with the coming of Spring. The first blossoms had now bloomed on their branches, and they shone ineffably as if they had been crowned with hundreds of thousands of laurels and garlands. Perhaps these were the signs of their respective good tidings which they hoped were bound to come.

So too did the children come out of their hidings for yet another season of fun, games, and play.

The same children, Shema's children, returned to him as surely and certainly as a river returns to the sea. They were unable to get enough, and in their reunion, there was an overflow of all those things that danced and were dearest in their hearts.

"Did you miss us?" shouted the children playfully, as they laughed and swayed around the tree.

Of course Shema did, and he bowed in his turn, offering the boys his flowers and the girls his fruit. And the children came together and prepared for themselves a lavish picnic in that special sanctuary underneath Shema's leaves, where they shared and exchanged all the goodness and beauty they had to offer. There the hymns of Nature began to sing so that truly one could say that Love was really in the air.

Meanwhile, as this was all budding, Iver looked on disturbed and in discontent. He had conserved all his energy, had expended all his force, had retained all his vitality, exactly for this moment, so that now when he flowered, his fruits and petals were so wonderful, so magnificent, so marvelous, so luscious, so other-worldly, that they were nothing less brilliant than all the Faberge eggs molded together and combined. And Iver smiled to himself and declared proudly:

"I am all that I am!"

Despite his bold claim, he could not escape his problem for the children returned, although not joyfully but with malice and revenge painted on their faces and feeding in their hearts. Had this tree not deprived them of their warmth in the Winter? Now, seeing it bud, it was their turn to deprive it of its glory in the Spring.

They all laid their eyes avariciously on a single piece of Iver's fruit that stood out among the rest, unlike anything they had ever seen. Larger than any watermelon or pumpkin, this fruit even weighed down the branch it was hanging from. This, they each thought to themselves, will be mine. That was only fair and proper they thought. Right?

Iver noticed something brewing though he knew not what. Besides, why should he care? Had he not withstood and overcome them each and every season before? He felt indestructible.

The children danced their dances, sang their songs, and played their play, except this time, it was not the same. For they were all preoccupied as to how they could steal that lovely and precious fruit for themselves. And now, the truly terrible game had begun.

The biggest of the group walked up to the tree, threw a rope around the branch on which that fruit hung, planted, and dug his feet into the ground, and began to pull. He heaved and heaved with all his might, but the branch did not budge, let alone did the piece of fruit even sway, despite his best efforts.

Iver laughed maliciously as he shook him off.

"After everything that has transpired, do you really think you can take my fruit? Beat me? Overcome me?"

But his voice went over their heads. Obviously, he thought since he was so much bigger, taller, higher, better than them.

The children whispered among themselves. This was a matter to be dealt with by them all since they were all affected, since they had all been pitilessly ridiculed, mocked, and shamed. Slowly, one after the other, the children went up to the tree where the boy was standing, grabbed a coil of the rope, and prepared to do battle in this now very real and heated tug-o-war.

Together they heaved, and the branch swayed lightly, as if someone had breathed and blown on a flower. Progress they thought, but not near enough to threaten, let alone make Iver care. To him, this was the type of fun he could get around—seeing the children suffer him.

Though the children tired, they would not be, nay, refused to be deterred. Rather than pulling the rope haphazardly as they had been, they coordinated and timed themselves to make a more concerted effort, pulling on the count of three.

"One, two, three, heave!" shouted one of the girls, "one, two, three, heave!" And they kept up their shouts and motions as if it was some battle cry leading them into war.

To the children's amazement, Iver wavered just as a tree should. Yet, it was nowhere near enough to bother him for it felt like a typical invigorating Spring rush of air through his leaves.

Not long after, the children's parents came out in droves, to see what all the huffing, and puffing, screaming, and shouting, kerfuffle, and guffawing was all about. They saw their children going back and forth with the tree, and each one felt deep inside that it would be wise and prudent to join in too. Perhaps they thought that this would get them back into the house faster, perhaps they thought they might be able to relive their former glory days, or perhaps they just wanted to be children again, even if it were to be just for a moment. So, they all hurried to the rope and the snake now tripled in size.

Together, they all heaved under the timed shouts of some of the parents, and as they pulled, Iver bent. Finally, he thought, a worthy challenge, and so as to not be outdone, he pulled, and tugged back.

Down, up, down, up, down, up, the tree went, the back and forth continuing like a seesaw that would not cease swinging.

"Damn this!" someone shouted.

"We need more help!" shouted another.

"Muster up anyone who will come!" yelled a third.

And so, children scurried off and before long returned with more a more people until it seemed that a legion had assembled

with a single, common, and shared lot before them. People threw more ropes around the branch and piled onto them to even them out until they looked like distinct streams of souls flowing and floating down the Styx.

"Heave! Heave! Heave!" came the shouts. They all pulled, and Iver bowed. The people cheered until Iver pulled back with all the might befitting of a tree. So viciously did he pull, that some of the younger children among them were shaken and lifted off the ground.

Left, right, up, down, back, and fourth, they all went, and the longer the struggle persisted, the more they all concentrated their energies on winning this single fruit to the point where it blindly overcame them, consumed them, devoured them.

As the people pulled, they could feel their hands blistering and slipping on the rope from their sweat and blood. By now, they were sunburnt and calloused, breathing heavy, perspiring, on the verge of tears, and very ready to give up. Yet they did not. Something deeper corrupted them, drove them, urged them on to endure. And in this sick suffering was contained the seeds of their own destruction.

As Iver pulled, his roots slowly began to untie and come undone. He could feel himself fracturing and being torn apart ever so slightly, yet nonetheless, more and more. In spite of that, he too continued to pull, motivated by that same poisonous, contaminating, and infectious disease.

A creak was heard.

Now a crack.

With a final united effort all the people pulled the tree to the point where it was half hanging over them, almost completely uprooted out of the ground. They could smell the fruit, touch it, a few of them could almost even taste it, they were so close.

"This is my fruit!"

"My fruit!"

"No! It's my fruit!"

"Mine!" they all shouted ruthlessly.

But right at the point where the tension was most extreme, Iver pulled back with one final, calamitously savage, and unnaturally futile pull. The fruit exploded out of the people's hands, out of Iver's branches, and propelled high up into the sky like a boulder out of a catapult, into the very far distance. All their heads turned in unison, watching the fruit traverse through the sky as if it was some impossibly dazzling shooting star.

Iver so violently convulsed, like a mad dog shaking himself dry from an ungodly wet. All his leaves withered and fell, his branches shivered and sunk, and his trunk now barren and lifeless, shriveled into itself until it disintegrated. The tree seemingly disappeared and all that was left on that plot of land was a limp, shell of itself excuse for a trunk in the form of a stalk that was no larger than a reed.

Having resisted so fiercely, so intensely, so freakishly, the force of his destruction now caused all the people to collide, crash, and come apart in every direction like rotten and dead fruit. And as they woke up, came back to their senses, and collected themselves, they all departed empty handed, begrudgingly, wondering what had come over them, what had taken over and possessed their hearts, what had just occurred.

They could not remember what they had been fighting for, what they had so desperately been struggling with, what they had so wanted to cling hold of. Whatever it was, it must have been something of immense, tremendous, infinite value given how much they struggled. Yet, perhaps not valuable enough for they all walked away, amnesic, unfeeling, and numb.

Was this all worth it? How much had it all cost?

Alas, Shema found himself isolated and friendless. "Iver . . . Iver" he ululated into the night. But his words echoed painfully amidst that deafening sound of quiet. He looked over to the place where Iver once stood. Iver was so spoiled, so annihilated, so ruined that it was not clear, nor could he tell whether whatever remained was shielded and protected by him or had vanished and been swallowed up in his shadow, lost to oblivion, to eternity.

Shema now stood by himself, all alone. And so ended the first conference of the trees.

THE BOY AND HIS ROD

"Every true gift is none other than a flame of love."

—Sophrony of Essex.

In the days of the Pharaohs, in the lands of sandcastles, a beautiful boy was born who would indelibly leave his mark on the world. By the ripe age of six months, it had become abundantly clear that his parents neither wanted him nor were willing to raise him. So, they wrapped him in extra cloth, placed him in a woven palm basket, and set him sailing down the river with the fraught and pitiful blessings of people who have nothing left of themselves to give but apathy and ennui.

It just so happened that at that time, down the river, an old, barren spinster was bathing. Seeing the basket float by making peculiar sounds, she could not resist swimming out to it, taking hold of it, and pulling it to shore with her.

To her surprise or horror, she found this baby, but it was neither screaming nor crying, rather it was abnormally groaning or ululating in such a broken, spasmodic way that the deepest of her maternal feelings were most naturally aroused. It was as if the child, though almost breathless, was calling out to someone. It was not his parents nor was it anyone else that had forsaken him in this life, rather it seemed he was calling out to someone else he had known, someone he had known intimately, someone he had known even before he was born, and now wished to be recalled and re-joined to.

The old spinster took the baby in her arms and quietened him. A peaceful look of content shone on its face as if their union was destined to be. In the calm, she looked up to the sky and thanked God for all her blessings. She looked back down at the child, and it smiled upon her, filling her with a warm, cozy light. She raised the child above her head, and aloud, she called out:

"To you Lord, I dedicate this boy, your servant, Daniel."

Years passed from that day, and the boy grew and came into fruition, under the watchful and diligent care and guidance of the spinster, who he called "mother." There he learnt and was raised in such a way that soon he came into the acme of his youth. He became loyal, devoted, and hardworking to her, yet hardly was he ever content or satisfied with anything, most of all himself. Though he was uneducated, something deep inside of him stirred, forcing him to look elsewhere, and pulling him far away. He could not help but long and thirst for this other space, and being in a desert he desperately sought some kind of nourishment so that this niggle might be quenched and fulfilled.

Every night, under the stars, the spinster would find him gazing out towards the land of sandcastles, if only to take them all in. He was always rendered speechless before those idols and could only sigh heavily under their crushing weight. One night, seeing him this way, she could not help but ask:

"What's troubling you, my boy?"

But the boy could not speak. He stayed silent, for he had not the words, nor the knowledge, nor the experience, nor the understanding to truly express himself and all his desires.

The spinster looked at the sandcastles on the horizon and intuitively knew what plagued and troubled him.

"This here is not enough for you. You want more?"

The boy nodded. "The sandcastles tempt me, entice me, pull me in."

The spinster laughed a hauntingly beautiful laugh, fitting for all her years and experience, a laugh that seemed to come from outside of her, beyond her, a laugh that smirked and taunted the boy and got under his skin.

"Why do you laugh at me mother?"

"I don't. I'm not."

"Then why are you laughing?" he asked, still unaware, "I tell you mother, one day I shall be numbered among them all?"

"And then what?"

"Then, they shall come to know me, and love me, and glorify me," said the boy, "and one day they might even bow down to me too."

"And one day you shan't be no more, and on that day, you shall have to account for it all."

"Do you not believe in me mother?"

"Far from it, dear boy. It's not that."

"Then what is it?" asked the boy, almost fed up with his mother.

"You must learn that there are things far more valuable and precious than that in this world, things that are priceless, and cannot be bought, even with all the entire world's gold and riches."

"Like what?"

The spinster simpered, and that simper rang out into the night. "I can't answer that for you. You must live it, and learn it, and judge it for yourself."

The boy seemed troubled by these vague and cryptic words. He expected his mother to continue but she did not. Instead, she smiled a soft smile that felt like a hug in his heart. She placed her bony hand on his tenderly, tracing little circles, and spoke as openly, genuinely, and heartfelt as one would during a confession, laying her soul completely bare before him.

"Take your mother's advice now that she's in her old age: guard yourself. It's one thing to be tempted and fall . . ."

The boy clung onto her words as they filled and lingered about in the stillness like incense. She continued:

". . . it's another thing to stay there and not dust yourself and get back up."

That night, both mother and son slept under the heavens. When morning had come, the boy awoke refreshed but found that his mother had passed, having breathed her last. The boy grieved but did not let Grief consume and devour him. He endured it bravely, and having made the necessary arrangements as best he could, he buried his mother and celebrated her life once more, all the while cherishing that hauntingly beautiful laugh, he thought he could seemingly still hear. Now, all alone in this world, with no one to love but himself, he set out for the land of sandcastles in the hope of making something of himself, for himself, something that might even outlast him.

After wandering for so long through the desert to the point where his faculties began to fade in the heat of the noontime sun, the boy saw what appeared to be a dry, lifeless bush, full of splinters and twigs, ablaze and burning with a pale, green flame. He staggered to what he thought was a desert haze, and as he got close, he fell, blinded by its light.

"Arise, Daniel!"

The boy arose, trembling. "Here I am. But how do you know me?"

"I am!" the burning bush boomed.

Those words echoed thunderously, and the boy hid his face because he was afraid, lest something should happen to him.

"Daniel, take off your sandals, for this place is a holy place, and draw near to me."

The boy obeyed, and as he approached, he felt a cool, gentle breeze emanating from the green fire, contrary to all his senses and unlike anything he had ever felt before. Just like that, he was reinvigorated and restored, as if somehow, he had been injected with new life, with more life.

"Verily, I tell you," continued the burning bush, "I have chosen you so that you might build a great nation right here, in this very spot, and deliver its people."

"But who am I?" said the boy, "who shall listen to me, let alone, come here to this wilderness and desert."

"A time is coming when these sandcastles, under the mirage of their own immortality, will fall, and the people will flee to you, in a mass exodus, and you shall act in *my name*."

"And suppose they don't believe and obey?"

"Are you faithful?"

The boy was silent.

"Daniel, put your hand into the bush and lift up its root."

The boy's hand wavered and almost went limp as he tried to move it to the bush. He had to muster up everything, all of his strength, all of his very being, to make his hand move, let alone, obey. Once inside the fire, neither did his hand burn, nor was it consumed. In fact, quite the opposite occurred, for in this fire, his hand became stronger and more powerful, like steel after a furnace, and he pulled out the root. His eyes moistened and became misty.

As he removed his hand from the fire, the burning bush asked, "what is that in your hand?"

No longer did the boy hold a root. Rather it had transfigured into a mighty rod that could easily support him. As he beheld this, the boy was profoundly moved. He gripped it in his hands powerfully and waved it mightily above his head.

"Cast the rod to the ground," the burning bush now said.

The boy obeyed and the rod became a scaly serpent that slithered and hissed aggressively at him, causing him to panic and make to flee.

"What is this?" the boy screamed out, terrified.

"Reach out your hand and grab the snake by its head."

"I can't!" cried the boy.

The burning bush repeated itself, even more forcefully than before, and this time the boy had no choice but to obey, even if it was reluctantly.

"Are ye of such little faith Daniel?" the burning bush blasted.

The boy reached out and caught the snake by its head. As soon as he held it firmly in his hand, no longer did the snake hiss because it had transformed back into the rod again.

The boy was so touched, so affected, that he could not bring out any words to say. "How can I doubt anymore?" he thought, and yet the burning bush heard his thoughts and knew them, even before the boy himself thought or was even conscious of them.

"Verily, I tell you I am the Lord of the Living."

The boy fell to his knees and bowed his head before the burning bush. It went on:

"Daniel, you shall found a kingdom, here and nowhere else, *in my name*, because of your faith, made active and true by your love, and I shall raise and exalt it above all the nations."

"And if I can't?"

The burning bush angered.

"Why do you still doubt me? Go! You shall do all these things through He that strengthens and endows you."

And just like that, in a most magnificent and extravagant flash, the flame extinguished and evaporated into itself and all that was left was the original bush. Except now, the bush was no longer dry, barren, and lifeless as before, rather it was thick and full, with luscious deep green shrub and foliage, though it was in the heart of the desert. It was at this spot that the boy would build his house to serve as a means of praise and a constant reminder of all that he intended to do.

Over the next weeks, the boy set about building a house at that spot, in the middle of the desert, that he might call "Home." Though simple, the boy built a silt dwelling that satisfied him for now. Here he passed his days in an ever-increasing loneliness born of his belief that he had been tricked, misled, and forsaken. In his despair, the boy would often cry out, and though no one would come, he seemed to feel a hand hold him firmly and remind him ever so softly to "have patience, my dear."

One day, a wanderer stumbled upon his house and collapsed before his door. At the sound of the loud thud, the boy ran to see what had happened. The wanderer lay motionless on the floor, having fainted. His skin was dry and cracked so that he looked more like a lizard than a human being.

The boy's heart panged, so he lifted the wanderer and carried him inside. He tried to nurse him better as best he could, fanning him with a loose cloth that happened to be lying about.

Soon after, the wanderer woke up abruptly in a panic, choking and heaving.

"Water! Water!" he managed to gasp and splutter out.

The boy had none. He had run out and had yet to go out again to fetch some more.

The wanderer reached out and lightly took hold of the boy's hand. It felt like splintered wood.

"Help me! Please!" he managed to utter aloud.

The words rang out like an eagle and seemingly settled on the rod that had been placed to rest on the wall. The boy looked over and felt a desire, almost not of his own will, to aid him. Instinctively, he went outside and when he returned, he carried a large stone in his hand. He laid the stone before the wanderer who was lying on a mat, picked up his rod, and struck it at the navel.

The stone cracked as a coconut might, and the boy picked up both halves and gave it to the wanderer. The inside of the stone had hollowed out like a cup, and a pool of crisp, crystal-clear water swelled about, which the wanderer was beyond thankful for.

He drank and drank and drank without hesitation, without even comprehending what had occurred, as if this was the most natural and ordinary of things to satisfy himself fully. And when he stopped, the water had finished so that he drunk just exactly as much as he needed to be properly satiated and sustained.

Instantly, the wanderer leapt to his feet, refreshed, and rejuvenated, as if he had drunk from the wellspring of Life itself, and thanked the boy whole-heartedly for all that he had done for him.

The boy was still in shock and disbelief. All he could mumble was, "don't thank me, thank Him that works through me."

The wanderer merely laughed and brushed him off saying that he best be on his way. But the boy pleaded with him to stay and help him build his city, a city which he said would surpass all the sandcastles he had seen and would ever see, just as he had been foretold.

If the wanderer was already laughing, at this, he could no longer contain himself. "A city in these desert sands? Now it is you who is hallucinating and going crazy. Such a city can never be," he said bursting out.

"But did you not see what I did for you?"

The wanderer was confused.

"You gave me water," he said after a moment in the most natural and matter-of-fact tones he could have, "yes, you gave me water."

With that, the wanderer departed for he had no reason anymore to hang around, leaving the boy to question everything he had just experienced and seen. He could find no answer to this Sphinx. Instead, all he felt was a voice deep inside him that seemed to say, "patience, my dear. Live the mysteries."

Again, weeks passed, and though lonely, the boy contemplated, impressed, and contented himself with his rod—his newfound power. As the time went on, he idolized it more and more until he began to be totally swallowed up by his belief that because he was such a great and powerful man then undoubtedly, only he could be worthy of such a great city to go along with his status and way of being. This, he thought, was only natural, right, and fitting, especially now that he had his almighty rod that he thought signified such.

One day, a traveler stumbled across his house. Screaming to be let in, he banged on the door so viciously and violently, that the boy thought that whoever this person was, was going to kick the door in and take him away. But this notion did not threaten and take too much hold over him, because the person kept repeating manically, "food! Food! Food!"

The boy opened the door, and there standing before him was a half-crazed, ravaged man who looked more like a beast, hungrily looking at him.

"Food! I need food!"

The boy looked him up and down. His odor wafted, filling his senses and he immediately became stand-offish and repulsed. He answered, "I can't help. I'm not sure I can spare anything for you."

But the traveler would not be deterred. He would do anything it seemed to eat.

"Feed me!" he kept exclaiming in such a menacing way that the boy could not help but think that if he did not concur then surely, he would be feasted on instead.

Again, the boy now felt a burning desire to help, as if someone had seared and branded it within him. He ushered the traveler inside to his table, where he took up his rod and tapped a scrap of bread that had been left on it. What he hoped would happen he did not know, but behold, he saw it transform into a whole, large, warm, fresh loaf. The boy broke off a small piece for himself and gave the rest to the traveler so that he might eat.

Greedily, the traveler scoffed it all down without so much as a care or concern in the world, and when he finished, not only was he satisfied, but was filled to overflowing on that bread of Life, the best bread he had ever tasted. With food now in him, the traveler softened and began to talk and express himself more easily and freely.

"Thank you, dear boy. I was trying to go to the land of sandcastles but got lost on my way. I have been wandering, lost for days on end, to the point where I thought that I should die. That is until, by some chance or miracle, I came across you."

"I suppose it's the least I could do for you," replied the boy.

"Well, I thank you again. I shall rest a little, and then if you were to be so kind as to point me to the land of sandcastles, I shall best be on my way."

"Why do you hasten to leave so quickly?"

"Where else shall I stay? Where else can I go?"

"Stay with me," the boy now said in an unusually quiet, strained, and pleading voice.

The traveler merely stared at him vacuously. "Here?" he exclaimed but could not continue because he was bemused. Having recovered himself, he spoke again, "there's nothing for me here."

"But I am to build a great city, even greater than any of the cities in all the lands of the sandcastles," the boy proclaimed proudly.

"And how shall you do that?" the traveler replied, shaking his head at him with pity.

"Why with my rod. Did you not see what *I did* for you?"

"You gave me bread," said the traveler most assuredly, trying to dispel his confusion. "Yes, you gave me bread."

With that, the traveler too departed, leaving the boy all alone to struggle with himself. "How could they not see?" he thought to himself, and the months passed with him hung up on this question, the quiet loneliness and desperation creeping over him ever so slightly more and more until his faith had almost totally dwindled because of the lack of visible signs and manifestations of this supposed great city. Right at that lowest point, when he was about to give everything up, the earth around him began to tremble and shake, and the sand came up in a rough, whirlwind frenzy.

The boy could hear the seismic din and clamor of thousands of feet, hooves, and voices getting louder and louder, until tribes of people began to emerge from the dust storm before his house. They began to wonder and marvel at seeing this desert hermit, believing him to be something of a saint, a madman, a lunatic, a beast—in other words someone unlike them, someone totally foreign and different, someone he was not. Inspired and moved, they began to praise and revere the boy, seeking his counsel, for they were new here.

As more people emerged, murmurs, and whispers coursed through the crowd as they questioned who this boy was and whether he would help and save them. Soon, people began to hush others as they waited expectantly, until a deathly silence descended upon them, like a panther in the night, as they faced the boy off.

All of a sudden, the boy raised his hands to them and spoke aloud.

"Have faith in *me*. Stay with me and *I* shall build you a city, greater than any city in all the lands of sandcastles, and *I* shall raise you above all nations."

The crowd, like Thomas, doubted and then a multitude of voices swelled up and began to chant aloud repeatedly, "prove it! Show us!"

The boy picked up his rod, lifted it above his head and made one swift motion. He drove the wind through and out of the crowd so that it quelled, parted the dust, and even settled the sand on them. Then, in another grand gesture, he drew a cloud over them and made it drizzle, if only to wash and cool them as proof.

"Can you not see who *I* am? What *I* can do?" the boy proclaimed, "stay and *I* shall build you the greatest of all cities and kingdoms."

All the people looked on, filled with fear and awe. From hushed and low voices arose and ever-increasing tumultuous exaltation that burst forth like successive tidal waves and surges of praise and worship.

"Savior, save us! Savior, save us! Savior, save us!"

The boy was deeply affected and wounded by all their shouts and cries, whether he was conscious of it or not. He remembered all that had happened to him, all that was pronounced to him, and now, standing on the cusp of the fulfilment of this promise, somewhere deep inside his heart and mind, he really believed *he himself* was to be their savior and deliverer.

The people now all gathered around him and set about building this great city in the weeks and months that followed. During this time the boy would walk ravenously with his rod like a shepherd through his flock, weaving in and out, and through and about his people lending his powers to them as he saw fit.

"Please sir," said an aged man on one occasion, stopping the boy by grabbing his tunic. "I'm old and have a family of twelve. My hands no longer work well. Help me erect a house to shelter us."

The boy answered, "of course I can, but what shall you do for me?"

"What is it that you desire?"

The boy smirked and shrugged him off. "I shall grant you this, old man, but remember that *it was I* that helped you."

The boy lifted his rod and banged the ground three times with it as if he was knocking on a door. The ground answered, and from it sprang fourth a house just perfect enough for the family to fit in. Seeing this, the aged man fell to his knees and bowed before the boy.

"Bless you sire, now and always."

"Rise!" said the boy pompously, "let me have an offering to mark your dedication before I depart."

"But I have not the means to pay, sire?"

"Not the monetary means to pay," the boy corrected, as he admired the aged man's daughters salaciously, as one might a trinket among others that would do for this moment before they would inevitably be discarded later on for the next.

"I shall pick from among your daughters instead, to satisfy your debt to me."

The man tried to protest but the boy would hear none of it. He pointed to two of the girls and said:

"These two will do. They both shall serve me together."

The aged man refused to part with and give up his daughters, and seeing this opposition, the boy turned him to stone with his rod. Gloating in his crushing triumph over them, he called out so that all might hear:

"Are you all so insolent to forget already who I am? What I have done for you? Keep this statue as a reminder so that you don't ever forget."

And the people cowered from the boy, having not the spirit to stand up, protest, or even fight against him.

Occurrences such as these were not only frequent but by now, had become so common and customary that they were considered the norm. Impressed by the boy's power to facilitate and alleviate, though hesitant to give up such dear parts of themselves to him, people painfully and unwillingly parted with horses, heirlooms, money, precious stones, family members or anything else of value in order to satisfy and appease the boy's ever-increasing hunger and craving to be duly and justly compensated for what he deemed *he* had done for them. So much so, that soon the boy had amassed such a fortune that in the heart of the desert, he had built the greatest of cities, and a sandcastle that towered above all the others which housed the boy and was only suitable to glorify and serve him, and him alone.

So wonderous did this new city become, that people came from all the corners of the earth to see it, and its ruler for themselves, since nothing like this had ever existed or had been known before. But like all sandcastles, no matter their size, something someday will come to spoil and sweep them away.

The more the boy prided, lusted after, and even favored himself, the more his rod began to rot and become scaly, and what was once high, good, and noble, now began to falter, pervert, and wane. Instead of inspiring awe and faith in Him, the one who strengthens all, people became jealous and avaricious having had a taste for things that they could not, nor were permitted to have for themselves. Though the boy could see this, still he did not care because he had his rod, the power to restrain, subdue, control, and ultimately dominate them all. And in such a tangle, how quickly do things become undone.

One day, the boy happened to be walking through his city and came across a ragged child, barefoot and in tattered clothes, musing to himself. The boy could not help but overhear him.

"Ah, to have a sweet today would be so lovely," Solomon (for that was his name) said dreamily.

The boy stopped before him and looked down upon Solomon. He interrupted him, speaking with a feigned and capricious benevolence that all the people had now become accustomed to:

"And should *I* grant you a sweet, what sweet would you like?"

Solomon paused for a moment, pondering thoughtfully, before responding almost musically, "if you should be so kind, I would ask that you surprise me."

"And were I to do so, what shall you give me in return?"

"What should you like? I have nothing," said Solomon, earnestly.

"Don't lie to me," said the boy harshly, "everybody has something. Do you not want your sweet?"

"Not if it should cost me so dearly," said Solomon innocently.

At this, the boy became incensed. Who was this child who dared to cross and challenge him? He lifted his rod to strike Solomon and turn him to stone, to teach him a lesson, but as he did so, the rod turned into that same snake, jumped at the boy, and sunk its teeth into his neck.

The boy winced and withered and fell flat onto the ground just as surely and certainly as Ozymandias and all the other rulers did before him. He sizzled and convulsed in the heat of the desert sun slowly as his life expired from him until he was dead, all the while he heard again the hallowed, echoing music of that hauntingly beautiful laugh.

As the boy lay there, lifeless, and still, the snake coiled on his chest. It held up its head and hissed so that no one dared go near the boy, as if he was guarding or protecting some hidden treasure. Undoubtedly, this was a sign. In spite of all the lengths that the boy had gone to, to assert and stamp himself on the world, he was so powerless that he could not even die with his rod.

His body began to fester and decay and not long after, worms began to crawl out of his eyes and mouth and chest and fingers. He had been eaten alive, from inside and out, so that now it was clear that not only was the boy dead, but was totally obliterated, annihilated, and vanquished, in front of all to see. Word spread and people came to look upon their once ruler and satisfied that his power over them was broken and that he breathed no more, they packed up what little belongings they had left, and departed from this wretched city for the next sandcastle land they might find.

Now that everyone had gone, the city was hollow, empty, and forgotten like all the other sandcastle cities of old. But it was not dead.

Solomon still roamed the streets, for even after all these years, he still had no place to go. Yet strangely, in this ghost town he saw "Home," something that he could make his own.

Now alone with the snake, it stopped hissing and calmed in Solomon's presence as if before an old friend. He felt sorry for the animal, so he bent to pick it up, if only to nurse it and set it free. As he did so, the snake turned into a rod, and his heart trembled.

He was not scared, rather something had moved him, inspired him, compelled him to act.

Solomon lifted the rod to the sky to examine it. Before the sun, it blazed and became inflamed, gleaming with a white-hot, glowing, and searing light. He lowered it, and down came all the houses and buildings. He had levelled the land, and now sought to create and bring to life something fresh and new for all to enjoy and partake in, if they were willing to.

Solomon looked at the rod. Though he might have wielded a great power, he had no need or desire for such temptation. What use would that be for him? He wanted to make and build something with his hands for himself and dedicate it to others that he might come to meet and know. So instead, he dug a hole and buried the rod, like one who plants a seed, not for himself but for a future generation. He then set about making a humble silt house for himself where he might begin to live.

As he labored, it seemed to grow darker and darker and a great shadow came upon him, though he could be sure it was still day. He did not mind too much since the shadow cooled and calmed him. Eventually, curiosity got the better of him, and so he turned to look. There, standing before him, on the spot where he had just buried the rod, had grown and blossomed a mature, lusciously rich fig tree.

Solomon picked a fig off the tree and smiled. He sat in the tree's shade, felt the gentle, fresh breeze from its leaves rustle through the curls of his hair, and dance and sway on his skin, all the while he enjoyed the sweet, juicy nectar of the most delicious treat he thought there could ever be. There he sat faithfully, enjoying his own company but open and willing to share a fig or his home with any stranger that might come past whether for a night, or for the rest of his days.

HANZ

"Believe me, nothing on earth is given without labour, even love, the most beautiful and natural of feelings."

—LEO TOLSTOY.

ANTIGONE WAS JUST LIKE every other child her age. She rose early with the sun and went to sleep with the moon and the stars, and in the hours in between, tried to pack her days with as much fun as she could. She dreamed and imagined, whether it was night or day, and in that way, she dwelt and moved intimately in both the earthly and the divine realms. Her fancies were so grand that when she let her parents in on them, they could not help but laugh in sheer wonder and amazement, profoundly moved by the fact that their child was blessed in such a way.

Antigone would laugh too, though she did not really know why. She felt that if her parents laughed, then she should too, together with them. There must have been something in that laughter that was so infectious because of how quickly it unfurled and spread.

When Antigone had finished up with these matters, she would then return to wondering. Really, however, two thoughts seemed to constantly occupy her mind: first, what fun would she get up to today, and secondly, what would she be when she grew up. In some strange way for her, the two seemingly went together, hand-in-hand, like sweet, little lovebirds. This was because, though she did not know exactly what she wanted to do, she knew above all else that whatever she did do, she needed to be inspired and fulfilled. In other words, she needed to be able to dream and have fun. And that was how her two thoughts magically intertwined and melded together.

What caused Antigone to have the most fun that she might grow up to be involved in such a thing, you ask? Tending to all her weirdly wonderful and delightfully distinct trees, plants, and flowers in her garden. A garden specially and specifically created and curated for her by her parents for this express purpose.

She derived so much joy and pleasure from her garden that she would declare innocently to her parents, "I want to be this flower or that flower when I grow up!"

"You mean a florist perhaps, darling," they would say encouragingly, "that might be more fitting."

And all Antigone would reply to that was, "sure, sure" absently, "whatever you say, so long as I'm with my flowers!"

And so being in her garden, her kingdom, was how she occupied almost all of her day.

Every morning, Antigone would wake up with the sun, right at that point where it winked on the horizon and would run out to welcome it in her garden. Why? Because she could resurrect and rise with Life itself each new dawn. This she determined was the best way to start her day.

Once there, she would sing and dance with her flowers as they wavered and swayed in the cool, crisp, morning breeze, and greet the birds, butterflies, and bees that would gather, dreaming that one day they too might respond back to her felicitations in words that she could understand, and not just in coos and trills.

After, she would make herself two jam and cream scones and a glass of warm milk, and she would sit in her throne, an antique, lacquered, auburn-brown deck chair, and admire the stunning, steady coming of Day.

When she finished her breakfast, from there, every day, she would sail the waves of Morning and skip across the rolling clouds as if they were stepping-stones of a majestic, cosmic hop-scotch game. And this day was no different for her. Except this time, for some unknown reason, while she was skipping, she tripped, stumbled, and fell face first into a cloud.

Whether she was seriously hurt or otherwise concussed she could not tell, for despite her best efforts to get up or even move, she could not, because she was firmly fixed and stuck to the floor. Antigone closed her eyes, and not too long after, she either blacked out or fell asleep to escape the terrible thought that she could no longer understand or make sense of her reality and dreams.

After a while, Antigone woke up with a muffled scream to the poke, poke, poke of what felt like a stick on her behind.

"S'cuse me, mizz, you alright?"

"I'm stuck," Antigone retorted, with her usual, characteristic sass, "can't you see?"

"I can see. I just didn't want to disturb you if you had stopped to rest, mizz."

"Well, I haven't," said Antigone with a huff and a puff, unable to see the voice talking to her, "I'm stuck. Are you going to help me up?"

"For sure, mizz, if only you'd ask."

"Don't be smart with me," cried Antigone, more and more frustrated because of her own dismay.

"Of course not, mizz, I'm just waiting for your words."

"Help me then!" Antigone exclaimed rather inexplicably rudely to this curious voice, before she added a kinder, "please," after a deep breath of reflection.

"There you go, mizz," said the voice, as Antigone felt herself being hoisted back up onto her feet again as a fish might feel being pulled out of the water on a fishing line.

She turned around to face her newfound companion, but to her surprise and alarm she found no one there.

"Down here, mizz," came the voice.

Antigone looked down, and there facing her stood a gnome with a scruffy beard, a pointed red cap with a white pom-pom on its tip, that matched the color of his hair, and a rake in his hand. Startled, she jumped back with a fright.

"Nothing to be afraid of here, mizz."

Antigone brandished her fists whimsically, trying to create with them two deadly weapons.

"Who are you?" she asked, with a voice that trembled and shook.

"I could ask you the same thing."

"And what are you doing here?" Antigone continued to babble.

"I could ask you the same thing," the gnome replied again.

Antigone became silent and thoughtful. She closed her eyes and rubbed them hard, hoping to whisk and wipe away the end of her dream. When she opened them again, she found the gnome still standing there. So, she collected herself in a way that all young ladies seem to do and decided to play along. She now spoke with a sure and certain sweetness that was becoming of her.

"I'm Antigone . . . but everyone calls me Tig."

The gnome bowed respectfully, seemingly enchanted by her charm and grace, for she was unlike anyone he had ever seen before.

"And your name?" Antigone asked politely.

It was the gnome's turn to blush and go silent. He looked at her attentively and then spoke in a voice whose pitch was slightly higher than before, betraying his sense of shyness and embarrassment.

"Nobody's asked me that before," said the gnome, "but . . . my name is . . . Hanz." And he pronounced it so particularly, in such a way and so similar to "hands" that Antigone could not be sure which was which.

"Hands?" Antigone asked curiously, with a slight turn of her head.

"No Tig, I mean mizz, Hanz."

"Forgive me, Hanz," said Antigone delicately, as she extended her hand to shake his warmly, all the while adding with a bright smile, "Tig is just fine."

"Well, the pleasure is all mine then, mizz Tig," said Hanz, putting his forehead in her palm and shaking his head, since he was unaware of her customs.

Antigone giggled, amused, "what was that?"

Hanz answered that that was how he was raised to greet new people. At this difference, the pair decided to acquaint each other in their customs and ways, since they were so foreign and unfamiliar. And with their introductions now out of the way, they became best friends forthwith, beaming brilliantly as they basked, and bathed in the morning light together. Soon however, Antigone's memories rushed back to her like a tornado. Her world became foggy. Everything was muddled and jumbled so that as she looked around, she could not recognise anything, and this cloudiness reflected in her vacuous eyes and on her brow.

"Is everything alright, mizz Tig?"

"Where am I?" Antigone asked hesitatingly, in a voice that showed that her head was somewhere up in the clouds.

Perhaps the air was thin today, or she had not yet properly acclimatized, perhaps she had even forgotten. Whatever the case, though perplexed by her sudden and sweeping confusion, Hanz gently reminded her.

"You're in Cloud Cuckoo Land."

If Hanz had said that she was "Away With the Fairies," or "At Wits End," then perhaps Antigone would have understood, for she had heard and knew of those familiar places before. But at "Cloud Cuckoo Land," everything became distant, overcast, strange, and hazy, and all she could stammer out was:

"What about my house? My garden?"

"I don't know what any of those things are," said Hanz, "but I can assure you that none of those things are here."

Hanz' words ran riot in Antigone's mind like little sillies. He seemed to sense this and tried to pacify the commotion by trying to ease her mind.

"I've seen you skipping past here every morning. I've always tried to get your attention and say hello, but you never seem to hear me. But today, I must have gotten lucky because for whatever reason, you stopped."

"But that . . . you . . . this . . . can't be real," Antigone sighed, shocked by her surprise, "this must all be nonsense."

"Nonsense!" Hanz exclaimed sharply, almost taken aback. He paused, letting the scene linger for effect. "There is still sense in nonsense, one need only look, and the proof of that is standing right before your very eyes."

"But—"

"No buts," said Hanz cutting her off. "Sense, nonsense, it all might seem tense or immense, but I promise it's thence . . . thus . . . no, hence," he added, all muddled up.

Antigone stood there, her mouth agape. She could not seem to understand his trail of thought, and no words came to aid her in her misunderstanding. Instead, she decided to walk around the cloud to see if she could familiarize herself or at least get her bearings, but this too even proved challenging because, as she was unaware, the texture of the cloud was surprisingly cloggy, as if she was walking through a mixture something akin to marshmallow, spider-web, fairy floss, and extra-thickened cream. After much struggle, she reached the edge and went to lean.

"Be careful, mizz Tig!" came a shout, "too much and you might topple over and fall."

Antigone hastened back with a fright. "So, I really am up in the clouds," she muttered in disbelief.

Hanz overheard and quickly replied, "I already told you that, mizz Tig, you're on a cloud. I don't know where else you think you would be."

Her reality began to hit her. She was assailed, brick after brick, and all she could do was gather them until she had enough to build an abode in which she could house her darling Dream. So drawn into her world was she now, Antigone fumbled about with her words trying to figure out and determine what everything actually meant. Finally, she managed to blurt out:

"How come I haven't seen any of this before?"

"I don't know, mizz Tig. Perhaps, it's because you see only with your eyes and not with your heart."

Antigone reddened as a rose might when it very first blushes in Spring.

"Don't be ashamed and beat yourself up mizz Tig, it's something we must come into, something we must build up, something we must properly develop and learn."

A faint, heartfelt smile began to creep from her lips.

"Even still, we don't make it easy for you," said Hanz.

"Why is that?"

"Because if it was easy, then no one would take the time to see what was *really* going on."

"There's just one hole in that theory . . ." started Antigone.

"That there is," Hanz nodded in agreement.

". . . most people don't want to see."

"And you tripped on it."

"Huh?" the pair cried out, simultaneously.

"What do you mean I tripped on the hole?" Antigone asked pressingly, with consternation.

Hanz was not shy, he was a proud gnome, so seeing an opportunity, he did not pass up the moment to relate his history, his story, a story he went to great lengths and permitted himself great liberty in telling, doing so theatrically as if it was a grand Shakespearean soliloquy. Hanz started:

"Have you ever seen a hole in a cloud? Of course not. And if you say you have, I shall say you are lying for it is very rare to see one, if at all. Why is that do you think?" said he, with a pompous gesture.

Antigone pondered but shook her head and shrugged her shoulders. She did not know. Hanz took a deep breath and continued, at first softly, and then with more and more gusto, almost frantically, as if his words were a mighty stallion that might run away from him.

"I'll tell you why. It is because for eons, Hanz has had the responsibility, nay, the duty, to close up all the holes in the clouds as they open, so children like you don't go tripping, slipping, and falling into worlds you shouldn't be in. For eons, Hanz has successfully fulfilled this duty such that he cannot remember a time otherwise."

"Until now," Antigone murmured under her breath, very naturally and matter-of-factly.

"Until you!" Hanz said, glaring at her.

Antigone shook. "I'm sorry, Hanz. I didn't mean to take you away from your cloud."

"It's done now. It doesn't matter," said Hanz, in reply. And snapping out of his dramatic trance, he reminded himself of the duty he so far had neglected since Antigone had arrived. He raced over to a hole that had been growing all this time and began to rake it so that it would close shut.

Antigone followed, though hardly as gracefully, and watched him from behind. She could not help but giggle because a cloud closing looked very similar to someone playing with and pulling hot, stringy, melted cheese.

"Is something funny?" asked Hanz as he turned to face her, after he got done closing that hole in the cloud.

"No," Antigone replied melodically, "it's just sweet that you care so much and do all this for your cloud."

"Not just this cloud," said Hanz satisfied, "but every cloud. They're all mine. I care about and look after them all."

"You do this for every cloud?" Antigone asked in awe.

This question frazzled Hanz. "What do you mean by *every* cloud? I know of fifteen clouds, twenty maximum. It's an honest day's work."

"No silly," said Antigone, "that can't be right. Everybody knows that there are as many clouds in the sky as there are sheep on land. After all, they reflect one another."

"That can't be true," a shaken Hanz declared, since it was the first time he had heard of such sorcery, "I don't believe you."

"But it is," protested Antigone, trying to assure him.

"It can't be! Otherwise, I wouldn't be a ruler, the keeper of the clouds. I would be a . . . a . . . slave, one of a potential infinite many, with no sense of free and independent will or choice," said a choked Hanz, gruffly.

"I am not a slave, am I?" he muttered under his breath to himself, gloomily. His head dropped and he hurried to get away from Antigone by going to rake a hole closed on the other end of the cloud.

Again, Antigone followed him, getting better and better at gliding across the cloud as if she was ice-skating (or really, cloud-skating I should say to be precise).

"I'm sorry Hanz, I didn't mean to offend you" she tried to say consolingly.

But Hanz did not turn around.

"Really, I didn't mean anything by it, I promise."

Again, Hanz refused to acknowledge her. He merely continued to rake.

"Will you turn and look at me," Antigone said stubbornly, with the stamp of her foot.

Hanz turned to face her. He looked up at her eyes but saw right through. He tried for some words but all that came out was a heavy sigh, so he gave up trying to talk to her and returned to raking and smoothing out some cloud in front of him, for that is what he knew best.

Antigone became childish at this affront. "Can you even hear me, you silly gnome" she yelled at him, and when he did not respond, she ripped the rake from his hands and threw it across the cloud, if only to make him bow to her and listen.

To take away his rake was like to take away his hands, and Hanz very quickly became wild and rabid like a hyena that was starved and had just taken notice of its potential prey. After recovering his rake, he recovered himself. He sighed a sigh of relief and began to breathe a bit easier and freer. He now felt safer and more secure again.

"Won't you say something, tell me anything, please!" Antigone finally wailed out beside herself, on the verge of tears.

"It's just . . . it's just . . . I think you're right. I think I might be a slave," said Hanz with a heavy heart. "They put me here to get rid of me, saying that I would have a kingdom and could rule over Mhe, Miself, and Eye."

"Whatever do you mean?"

"Listen Antigone" Hanz now said seriously, "gnomes play, they idle, they daydream. That's what they are known for. To do otherwise, is not to be a gnome. I know all those things and I enjoy them in their due time, but I've always wanted more. I wanted to do something, make something, build something that lasts, you know? Maybe that's why they named me so," he said with a sly, cheeky chuckle before going on, "but a volley of voices always shot me down—"it's too hard, it's too difficult, it's not worth it, it's too much, it's against your very being"—they would all say. And then we would just get frustrated, fight, and get stuck, unable to move here or there, until we went back to being 'proper' gnomes. Then one day, my gnomes packed me up and sent me away, for they had had enough of my dreaming too big. They told me go live in your Cloud Cuckoo Land, work there if you want to, do whatever, but it's your loss, not ours. And so, I left. And come to think of it, I haven't seen another one of those gnomes ever since."

Antigone listened to him intensely, savoring each word of his strange narrative and revelation. She could not help but wonder why there were so many gnomes back home.

"What do you mean by stuck?" she finally managed to ask gently.

Hanz thought for a moment before he replied.

"Frozen, unable to move, unable to grow, unable to be, you know, stuck. Perhaps they've passed on, fallen away," but he shook his head to rid himself of those thoughts and images.

"Fallen!?" Antigone suddenly exclaimed, as if this was her priceless Eureka moment, "yes they must have fallen from their clouds onto our land because everybody has gnomes that are frozen, fixed, stuck to their places in their gardens back home."

"Where?" asked Hanz, flabbergasted.

"Down there," said Antigone rushing to the edge of the cloud and pointing to the houses which opened up to them like a yawn, down below.

Hanz took a moment to himself as the realization began to seep in. All he could venture to say to comfort himself was, "I wonder what they are dreaming about from down there? Whether they long to be back up here?" But I'm not sure how much that helped him.

"So he's alone on the cloud," Antigone muttered to herself, as she shuddered because her heart hurt for him.

Hanz overheard and went to reply, perhaps even thankful for the distraction, though he had been over this before.

"I don't know how many times I have to tell you things. I'm not alone, mizz Tig. It's Hanz, Mhe, Miself, and Eye."

Antigone burst out laughing, "I don't know how you do it, but at least you can joke and smile about all this."

Hanz did not share in her glee, he merely looked on at her, bemused and unfazed.

Antigone noticed that Hanz was still in the dark and tried to enlighten him, "you know, because it's just you, you're by yourself, all alone."

That did nothing for Hanz. So Antigone repeated his words back to him aloud, emphasizing each syllable, "it's just *me, myself, and I*, don't you understand?"

"You called us Hanz?"

"What?" said Antigone.

"No I didn't."

"But we heard you," three tiny voices squeaked again.

"You're . . . not talking," said Antigone as she pointed her wobbly finger at Hanz. Confusion bounced all around the cloud like a ping-pong match gone awry. From underneath a fold in the cloud, Antigone saw three little gnomelets, with white beard fuzz and all, pitter-patter out of their hiding and into the safe haven of Hanz's shadow. Antigone knelt down to admire them, softly patting each one of them on their head like they were fragile little ducklings.

Seeing this, Hanz introduced each of them, his progeny, to her.

"Mizz Tig, I present to you Mhe, Miself, and Eye," and as he did so, they each in their turn, jumped in the air, somersaulted, twirled, and landed effortlessly with a bow and a wave of the hand, before her.

"So you weren't joking," Antigone said with a chuckle.

"Joke, mizz Tig, heaven's forbid, why should I do such a thing to you?"

"Because I thought you said that's what gnomes do?"

"Ah, but I'm not so sure whether I am that given my newly discovered history."

"Don't say that!" Antigone said, as she hit him playfully on the shoulder, "you're the best gnome that I've ever known."

Hanz bowed his head gratefully, savoring those words as he would savor seeing the birds or an airplane as they flew past, or closing a hole on his cloud. The two lingered, and then after their moment had passed, Antigone turned to the gnomelets, knelt, and asked, "what do you all do?"

"We work, we play, and we have fun, altogether," sung and chanted the three gnomelets in sync, as if they shared one mind and will, "and of course, we look after Hanz."

And they disappeared, rumbling, and tumbling about, caught up in their own fun and games to prove their point, albeit over the top if only for attention and to make a scene of it.

"Are they what keep you from falling?" uttered Antigone.

Hanz nodded meekly, "I suppose they do," before adding, "I appreciate them, this, even if the price of it is constant, hard work."

"Sometimes I feel like I have fallen, and am stuck, and it's hard work to get back up and go on," said Antigone earnestly, "but–"

"No buts . . ."

"Yes I know, sense nonsense . . . " said Antigone, beginning to trail off.

"No," said Hanz cutting her off. "I'm flattered that you listened to one thing at least, but I wasn't going to say that.

"Then what were you going to say?"

"Listen and I'll tell you. Think of it like this. Even though its labor, it's a labor of love, a labor that in due time will bring to bear an abundance of incomprehensibly sweet fruit, fruit that might one day even outlive both you and me. Now isn't that something?"

"How do you know? How can you be so sure?"

"I have tasted it."

"Well, I want to bring forth this fruit," Antigone declared somewhat jealously.

"That you can," said Hanz, "and very easily too. You just have to decide what kind of fruit you wish to bear."

"How do I do that?"

By now, the gnomelets had returned and were in stiches because of Antigone's troubles and concerns. Finally, they were able to control themselves and then they spoke.

"We can't tell you that mizz Tig, some people just know, some people take their lifetime to figure it out, some people never do. All we can say is that if you do what you love, then you will be sowing the invisible seeds so that magical tree might grow. And though everyone shares the same water, if you continue to cultivate it with love, it might eventually blossom, and then who knows what fruits might be brought forth, though we can never entirely know if fruit will come for sure."

"It's like a leap of faith," added Hanz, for good measure, "or should I say, a seed of faith."

Antigone stood there and shook her head as she reflected. She felt a warm, opaque light stream through her like a river returning to its source. As if inflamed, she began to burn brighter and brighter, until she almost became too much, though she was completely and utterly unaware.

"This is too much for us, mizz Tig, I think it's time you go . . ." Hanz began to shout out, blinded.

"But I don't want to," interjected Antigone.

". . . before you combust, burn, and swallow us up with you," Hanz managed to finish.

Antigone turned into herself trying to contain her light as she listened to his words. She dropped her head and sighed understandingly as she realized what was occurring. After a moment, she turned to Hanz once more and looked at him with gracious and genteel eyes, though they were still ablaze.

"Will I ever see you again? Can I come back?" she asked tenderly.

"Perhaps mizz Tig, perhaps not, who can know for certain with these things."

Antigone's eyes moistened. This was not the answer she was hoping for. Hanz saw this and quickly added encouragingly:

"But it was a pleasure having you, mizz Tig, and you will always be most welcome back if you ever find yourself here again."

"Yes, mizz Tig," said Mhe, Miself, and Eye together, "you would be most royally welcomed back, as our Queen."

Antigone looked away to gather herself. It was all too much, for there is no feeling worse than premature separation.

"Best be off now," Hanz said, almost reluctantly, as a lump, like coal, formed in his throat, "otherwise you mightn't go. Then what should happen to us all?"

Antigone went to protest but Hanz silenced her. Deep down she knew too. It had to be thus. What would her parents say after all, if she was away for too long? Hanz walked up to her, and they embraced. It was a searing, lasting hug that undoubtedly left its mark. Finally, they broke off, against all their wishes.

"Goodbye Hanz, I shall miss you."

"And I too, mizz Tig."

"Yes, and we three," said the gnomelets, not to be left out or forgotten.

And before Antigone even had time to think about how she would get off the cloud and leave, with an almighty motion, Hanz jumped and flicked her in the middle of her forehead and sent her flying off the cloud and falling back to the ground. Antigone tried to scream and shout. All she heard in response were Hanz's final words, "no buts, it must be hence . . . thus . . ."

That was the last she ever saw of him, for she closed her eyes and disappeared with the sun.

When she opened her eyes again, Antigone found herself back in her garden, sprawled out before her delectable flowers. Was this all a dream? Had she really been up in the clouds? On Cloud Cuckoo Land?

She roamed about aimlessly to see if anything had visibly changed, but nothing seemed out of place, nothing was out of the ordinary. The daisies were still daisies, the tulips were still tulips, the gardenias were still gardenias, and the camellias were still camellias, all left where they should be. Except this time, when she looked at them, though they were undoubtedly beautiful, something was out of place. They stood out awkwardly against the unkempt, weedy wilderness of the rest of the garden.

Antigone looked down, looked back up at the flowers and looked down at her hands again. They twinkled. Perhaps it was her reflection she saw in them, perhaps it was something else. Whatever it was, it inspired her for she instinctively knew what she needed to do. She set about her task, her toil, her labor of love, to reveal and bring out her garden, for she determined and understood that that was where its true beauty lay.

When she finished, she saw in the garden something inexpressible, something glorious, something fiery, ethereal, celestial, and divine. Her forehead and fingers began to burn, as if such beauty could be terrifying to touch and behold, and right at that moment she realized. She looked up at the sky, to the clouds, to the Heavens, and smiled knowingly. A new part of her had been revealed, and she was thankful for this knowledge, even if it hurt and left some searing scars.

Antigone's mother poked her head through the back door. She was about to call out but hesitated a moment. As she lingered, she saw Antigone's back, and the way she stood there holding and carrying herself in the sun. An indescribable feeling came over her like a gentle wave, showering her in the warmth and radiance she thought Antigone must have felt in that moment, a feeling all parents know too well when they see their children truly happy and fulfilled.

Antigone turned. She saw her mother standing on the threshold. She called out to her, trilling, "mum, mum, come and look at the flowers today."

Antigone always asked, and her mother always obliged. She walked over to the flowers, put her arm around her daughter, and together they admired, indulged, and even got lost in them, her little joys, her little loves. They were always beautiful and splendid, today, even more so, in a way incommunicable and unlike any other time before.

"I wish this moment would last forever."

"I wish we never stop making these moments so that this one doesn't have to."

The two, lovely ladies looked at each other and then to the flowers. Together, they each took pleasure in and enjoyed the fruits of their labors of love.

THE ANTIQUATED MIRROR

"And God said, 'love your enemy,' and
I obeyed him and loved myself."

—KAHLIL GIBRAN.

IN THE AFTERNOON'S GOLDEN fairy hour, just before evening ineluctably comes, when the light dawdled and spilled through those French windows of their living room, illuminating their auburn locks as if they had been blessed and adorned with celestial crowns, the three sisters were busy playing games that might have swept them away, making all the fuss in the world, to their hearts content.

At that moment, Phoebe had just finished making her cardboard scepter, and picking up her crown. She gathered her sisters as subjects before her, pulled out a chair, assumed her position on it above them, and prepared to regale them with sillies, fancies, and trifles of old. As the oldest sister, this was her privilege, nay, perhaps even her prerogative.

She cleared her throat and somewhat pompously began:

"It is my great honor to stand before you ladies as your queen . . ."

The twins, Natasha, and Ioanna, burst out giggling, but Phoebe would not be deterred.

"... and as your queen, I wish to rule, to assume responsibility over you ... to help you ..."

"Be careful up there, Phoebe!"

But Phoebe simply ignored those words and went on:

"... if you listen to me and obey me, maybe one day you might even become like me. But that depends entirely on you," she proclaimed boldly, pointing at each of them in turn with her scepter.

"Phoebe I mean it, be careful up there so you don't fall," said her mother, who was reclined on the velvety green couch, watching on distractedly.

"Okay mum!" Phoebe groaned. "Now where were we," she muttered to herself before she started again with increasing gusto. "Ah yes ... you shall serve me, and the more faithfully you do so, the more I shall be inclined to raising you up," she said gesturing grandly, "but again, that depends entirely on you."

Low and subtle murmurs began to break out between the twins. Perhaps they had become bored with this same old game, perhaps dissatisfied, perhaps they had even stopped listening altogether. Either way, they looked at each other instinctively, in a way that only twins can, and began to walk towards either side of the chair, crossing over each other here and there.

"Do you understand?" demanded Phoebe.

The twins said nothing. Though they had lowered their heads, they looked up at her enticingly.

"Do you hear me?" shouted Phoebe as they continued to approach even more ravenously than before, adding nervously, "what are you doing? Where are you going?"

Still the twins remained silent. Their revolution had already begun, and the force of this resolution could not but impel them onwards. They began to circle around the chair like a shiver of sharks.

"Why do you get to rule over us all the time?" Ioanna asked lullingly.

"Because!" stammered Phoebe, who was unable to verbalize what she thought was her divine right, in other words, the typical eldest sibling response to their authority being directly questioned and challenged.

"But that's not fair," declared Natasha coaxingly.

The twins began to poke and caress Phoebe, all the while she desperately tried to kick and smack their little hands away.

"Leave me alone, this isn't part of the game."

"Why? Don't you like it?" asked Ioanna, with feigned sweetness.

"Is it not fun?" Natasha added in turn.

And as suddenly as that, the twins grabbed each leg of the chair and slowly began to shake it.

"Stop it!" cried Phoebe repeatedly.

The twins laughed, at times salaciously, at times mischievously, as they called out tauntingly, "what's wrong? Don't you like it? We just want you to feel how we feel."

Soon the twins were shaking the chair so roughly that Phoebe could not help but slip, and she fell to the ground with a loud thump. The twins quickly departed the scene of their crime lest any evidence of their mischief might arise, leaving Phoebe alone to nurse her sores.

"Phoebe. I told you you'd fall."

"But–"

"No buts. That's what happens when you're not careful. I don't want to have to say I told you so again."

Meanwhile, the twins looked on, snickering. Phoebe burned. She bit her lip to suppress her rage. "Sorry mum," she said in a voice that clearly choked and held back all that pain.

Phoebe found her teddy and went to the window to comfort herself. She stared out, almost vacuously, as she stroked Bunny's ears, all the while contemplating the innermost parts of herself. At first, she seethed. "I hate them," she kept muttering to herself, "I can't wait to get my revenge. I just have to work out how." But the longer she sat there, allowing her desires for revenge to chew and gnaw at her, the more these feelings self-destructed and dissipated because soon there was nothing left to feed on or eat.

Instead, Phoebe was left with a heavy lump in her throat, a lump for want of understanding. All she could do now was question herself and ask why. "Why had the twins done that? Why did they not like her? Why?" But she could find no answer. Whatever she thought would not make sense to her at all. At this, her eyes moistened, and she went numb.

"Maybe it's me? Maybe I'm the problem? Maybe there's something wrong with me?" she managed to conclude aloud.

As the twins watched on, their eyes too became damp and misty as a profound sense of guilt overcame them. They did not know why. In fact, they could not tell you why they did what they did. After all, Phoebe was not all that bad to them. It was all meant to be a big joke, all part of the game. They could see Phoebe struggling, so they decided to change their tune and sing a different song.

The twins picked up their dolls and approached her in a similar way that mourners might approach a coffin.

"We didn't mean to hurt you Phoebs," said Natasha softly.

"Yeah, we were just playing," Ioanna quickly added, "we thought it would be fun and different if we changed the game."

Phoebe sighed, and simply turned her back on them.

"You see, we always seem to play that game," continued Ioanna.

"And so, we thought why not do something different this time," added Natasha, trying to justify their actions, "we thought there would be no harm in that."

Still, Phoebe did not stir.

"Please Phoebs," they said pleadingly together, "we didn't mean it."

Phoebe turned to look at them. The twins stood there with downcast doe-eyes, pouting sympathetically. She could not stay mad at them for long. They were, after all, her baby sisters. They loved her and looked up to her, and it was in Phoebe's power to forgive them, since she always thought she knew what was best.

"Fine!" Phoebe blurted out in that typical way, after a long drawn out pause that seemed to emphasise the very deep feelings that passed and were shared intimately between them, "it's whatever, anyways."

The twins quickly filled with joy, and Phoebe intimated a smile in return. Even though she cherished their reconciliation dearly, she did not want to appear too happy and pleased lest it would take the momentary power she had over them away from her.

And now, with their passion and friendship restored, Phoebe with Bunny, and the twins with each of their dolls began to play what would be a very sweet, frank, and intense game of House as such siblings often do. But as we all already know, when it comes to siblings, sweetness is very quickly lost to frankness and intensity for better or worse, and it is somewhere here in that well-meaning but conflicting place that things usually go awry. Yet, what is often misunderstood in the moment is that it is not because of some evilness or lack of love on the part of the siblings that cause things to go wrong, but rather because, perhaps more often than not, of a spill in their overabundance of love and deep feeling that cannot be tempered, contained, or controlled. If this is the case, when an argument arises and occurs, the siblings are overcome by a storm of competing emotions, and very seldom do they remember their underlying affection, and instead cannot help but lash out and overreact, as we shall see.

At that point, Phoebe had just finished tying a dazzling pearly-white bow around Bunny's head and combined with the violet silken dress with yellow sunflowers that the teddy wore, she could not resist showing off its exquisite beauty and elegance to the twins.

While the twins were struggling to glamorize their dolls like Phoebe, let alone keep up with her, Phoebe turned to Natasha and playfully slapped her on the arm, declaring:

"Look at Bunny. There's no way that your doll could ever be as beautiful and lovely as mine."

Feeling included in Phoebe's perceived attack, Ioanna turned at those words too. At seeing Bunny, the twins did not wish to be outdone so they retorted quite quickly in their own way, something to the effect of:

"We'll show you! Just you wait and see!"

And so began their next competition.

While the twins worked manically, almost furiously, to style their dolls, Phoebe quietly stroked and caressed Bunny's ears all the while whispering sweet nothings to it. She keenly waited in delightful anticipation to see what the twins might come up with.

"Voilà . . . I'm finished!" the twins soon proclaimed together, in due time, before they went about showing off their dolls just as Phoebe had done.

And while their dolls were indeed unique and special, in that wackily weird and absurd, childish, imaginative way, they in no way could compare to the rich, graceful sophistication of Bunny, that could only come about because of Phoebe's age and experience.

The twins seemed to feel and sense this, but nevertheless, Phoebe cooed at their work so as to not disappoint them, before adding boisterously, "they're charming . . . how cute."

But the twins were not impressed. Something was off, different. "Charming," and "cute", these were the words that Phoebe had used to describe their dolls, but not "beautiful," and "lovely." They slowly became incensed. "Why not beautiful and lovely? What was wrong with their dolls?" they thought to themselves, and the more they sat there, the more they turned a deep scarlet, until they could not help but chastise and berate Phoebe, if only to move that sting and burn off of themselves.

"Bunny isn't beautiful! She's . . . she's . . . sickly," said Ioanna maliciously, as she fumbled about to find the right words that might cut.

"And the bow, the dress, they're all ugly too!" said Natasha spitefully.

This deeply hurt and wounded Phoebe since it had come from so out of the blue. She thought it was totally unfair and uncalled for, and so, as to not be outdone or walked all over, she fired back with a surprising alacrity.

"Is that so! Well, your dolls' hair is not combed right, the choice of clothes don't match, and most of all, your style is childish, plain, rudimentary, and basic at best."

Perhaps because Phoebe's insults were so quick off their mark, perhaps because they were so tailored, so specific, so targeted, perhaps because she used a language that the twins were not too familiar with, or perhaps because of a combination of them all, the twins could no longer contain themselves and blew up. They screamed and fell upon Phoebe as if she were some wild prey. Though Phoebe could usually fend off one sister, in this instance, with such ferocity, two were no match.

But her person was not what the twins wanted to devour and tear to shreds. Ioanna grabbed the violet dress of Bunny, and Natasha grabbed the pearly-white bow, and together they pulled and yanked hard at them. Not to be trodden all over without a fight, Phoebe tugged back with all her might. But before long, there was a loud tear that immediately silenced the three sisters.

Phoebe held Bunny in her hand. Ioanna and Natasha held the dress and the bow in theirs.

"Give it back!" Phoebe snapped at them with the wrath of a thousand Furies.

The twins flinched and hesitated. The room seemed to get darker and darker as if it was going to cave in on them.

"Give it back to me now!" Phoebe shouted shrilly.

The twins went to give Bunny's garments back, but the damage was already done. Phoebe's tears were so obvious, so pronounced, and so clear, that as soon as she held the garments in her hands, she looked murderously at the twins, directly into their eyes, into their souls, and said in a slow, calm, chillingly cold voice:

"I am going to kill you both."

She lifted her hand to slap them. The twins screamed out frightfully, and right at that moment when she was about to rain down her blows and strike them, she was thwarted and forced to stop, dead in her tracks.

"Phoebe Grace Marie! You put your hand down right this instant!"

Phoebe turned. Their mother was now hovering over her menacingly.

"But mum!" Phoebe cried out, her tear-stained face on the verge of fresh tears.

"I don't want to hear it. You go to your room at once and think about what you've done."

Phoebe glared at the twins with a look of fire, daggers, and blood. They bowed their heads to avoid her scorching gaze, refusing so much as to even dare look at her. Phoebe lingered a moment, before her mother shouted at her again.

"Go! Now!"

Phoebe tensed and clenched her fists as she stormed off to their shared bedroom, ablaze. She burst through the door, slamming it shut behind her and marched to her bed. She caught a glimpse of herself in the antiquated, mahogany mirror. Something stirred deep within her. She shattered before it, now letting these new, hot, fresh tears flow freely.

There was something terrifying, bewitching, liberating about that antiquated mirror. It acknowledged her, recognised her, perhaps even empathized, and understood her. It saw her without spot or wrinkle or any such thing, fully, and without blemish. It reflected to her all that she was and all that she was not. It beheld her completely and stood before her without judgement or condemnation. And in that throbbing, lonely silence, the mirror did not shrink or shy away, nor did it hide or reduce the lofty weight of Being from her. It stood firm, reflecting the person that she was, and not the person she wished or thought she should be. It reminded her that *that* person standing in the reflection would always be there, and served simply as a choice, a potential, a hope, of what she might grow into and become.

Phoebe noticed herself in the mirror. She could see the way her eyes had reddened, and how her bushy brows had scrunched and curved. She could see how her eyelashes fluttered, and how they glistened and glimmered with drops of tears, almost like jewels. She could see how these droplets slowly rolled down her cheeks, leaving their translucent trail behind. She could see how her locks cascaded down the side of her face, masking all that she felt, and yet despite all of this, she could not help but smile shyly, through her tears, at the reflection. She still looked beautiful, in every sense of that word, perhaps even more so now. Never had she beheld a more magnificent sight than that which looked back at her, regardless of the circumstances, because in this moment she was so vulnerable, so raw, so real.

Phoebe blushed as she brushed the hair from her face behind her ear. So too did the reflection. She pulled a funny face now, and the same thing happened in the mirror.

Phoebe was on the brink of overflowing. She burst out into an almost uncontrollable giggle, and her reflection did so too, until their voices floated about the room like nightingales. The sounds were so contagious, so magnetic, and exerted such a strong charm and lure that Phoebe felt herself being whisked away by feelings she could not totally understand, let alone even grasp.

She lifted her hand and reached out to her reflection, and it mirrored her, seemingly calling out to her and beckoning her to draw near. If only she could touch her, the girl in the mirror, hold her, hug her, then maybe everything would not be so bad. This gave her hope, encouragement, and so Phoebe walked slowly towards her reflection.

As she did so, she looked from side to side to ensure everything was safe and clear. She did not wish to be embarrassed or humiliated again. Her reflection now seemed to have a sharper and more elongated nose, but this eluded her as she was too caught up in the moment to notice.

She continued approaching and the reflection, for the briefest of glimpses, screwed up its face and lips crudely, in such a way as to make a chagrin and grimace, before returning itself to its proper form so that it might not be given away.

Phoebe felt a pang in her heart but by now she was merely inches away from the mirror.

Right as her finger was about to touch the reflection in the glass, in the hopes that something valuable or significant might be revealed or imparted to her, her reflection grabbed her so extremely by the wrist and pulled her into the mirror, forcing her to trade places with it so that it could escape from its cage.

Phoebe was now trapped in the mirror as if it was a prison cell especially designed for her, and this goblin, in the form, appearance, likeness, and disguise of Phoebe, was free to terrorize and wreak havoc as it saw fit.

Phoebe screeched and banged on the glass but to no avail. All was silent in the room. The goblin simply laughed and smirked at her wickedly. Now she felt how it had for so long, desperate to break out and burst forth. Phoebe trembled, terrified by the thought that she was imprisoned, and worse still, seemingly without any means of escape.

The goblin ran from the mirror around the room mischievously and menacingly, pulling out sheets and pillows and throwing them on the floor, flipping tables and chairs, and even going so far as to smash a Lego set and snow globe. Perhaps it was running away from something to escape after so long behind bars, perhaps it was running towards something that it had longed for now that it was free, perhaps its destination was one and the same. Who could say? But whatever the case, it could not help but return to itself, in front of the mirror. Before long, the goblin ventured to the door, collected itself, and began to crystallize and give voice to all the dark and terrible thoughts Phoebe harbored and tried to squash inside her.

Phoebe stood helpless at this transformation. All she could do was look on.

By now, the goblin had tidied up its hair, patted down, and smoothed out its dress. It opened the door as gently as it could and immediately laid eyes upon the twins who were playing innocently with their dolls, debating how they could approach Phoebe and bring her back out to play again. They were missing her all the more, as all siblings usually do.

The twins heard the door hinges squeak as it was closed shut. They turned to look.

"Phoebs," they squealed together, excitedly, "we were just about to come and get you to play."

The goblin did not reply. It simply titled its head and smiled at them in a strangely affecting way.

"Come play with us," they called out.

The goblin strutted over and tried to enmesh itself as best it could in their game. Both Ioanna and Natasha presented who they thought was Phoebe their dolls, showing and describing how they had newly glamourized and beautified them. With a certain sprightliness, they asked whether this time, their dolls were better than before. The twins held their breath and waited for the response, expectantly.

The goblin examined the dolls quickly before brushing them off. It grunted its approval in a voice that was slightly deeper than what the twins were accustomed to. There was something obviously preoccupying it.

The twins seemed to take note.

"Phoebs, is everything alright?" they asked softly.

The goblin remembered itself and what it was trying to accomplish and achieve, so it attempted to gloss over its temporary lapse by mellowing out its voice and replying to the twins as sweetly as any goblin could.

"Why of course. Let me see that doll. It's . . . beautiful . . . lovely."

The words struggled to escape and straggled in the air, triggering the twins. They were unexpected, in fact, very much off-sounding.

"You've never said that to us before," said Natasha taken aback, "are you sure everything is alright with you?"

The goblin snarled. It took hold of Natasha's doll and brought it close to its chest. It looked from the doll to the twins then back to the doll. In a moment that passed as quickly and ominously as the first flash of lightning before a storm, the goblin's smile grew to an almost demonic proportion. It lifted the doll up and began to strike and rain down blows on Natasha's head, one after the other, all the while roaring.

"I told you I would get revenge! How do you like that now!"

Natasha screamed and shouted. Tears streamed down from her eyes with increasing intensity, all the while she desperately tried to protect and shield herself.

"Stop it, Phoebe! What's gotten into you. Stop!" Ioanna yelled at her, trying to pull who she still thought was Phoebe away.

And though she succeeded at first, the goblin soon shifted its focus and now began to hit her until she too started to cry.

"Did you really think I had forgotten about you? Did you both think you could get away with what you did to me?"

"We're sorry, Phoebe," the twins managed to vocalize aloud in between their sobs and struggles. As soon as they were able to break free from its clutches, the twins grabbed each other and ran into their room to escape this little demon.

The goblin followed them, though it took its time, prolonging and drawing out their frightening ordeal, if only to make a point so that they properly learned their lesson.

"That's right," it shouted after them, "run away, that woman, that witch, isn't here to protect you now."

The twins tried their best to bar the door so that Phoebe would not be able to get into the room and then set about arming themselves and hiding so they could protect and defend each other as best as they could. In the midst of this hellish chaos, they both saw a girl trapped inside the mirror, banging against the glass, gesturing, and screaming soundlessly, hopelessly, pleading for their help.

"Phoebe!?" they cried out in horror and alarm, for they could not quite understand, though they knew something was most definitely wrong. Something overcame them at seeing the young girl struggle helplessly, and they knew that they must do whatever they could to help and save her—the 'real' Phoebe.

The door rattled. The twins froze almost to the point of lifelessness. After all, what could they do?

The rattling increased, getting louder and louder, and more and more violent, until it seemed that the goblin had kicked the locked door in. It burst through in a fury. High above its head, it was swinging the same chair that the twins had pushed Phoebe off, with the ease of someone who might have been holding and twirling a whip. God only knew how it was planning to punish them with it.

The twins stifled their cries. In the direness of the moment, they somehow managed to muster up all of their courage. They stood their ground firmly, feeding off the strength that they were doing this for their sister, for *their* Phoebe.

The goblin brandished the chair. It hung above them all pervasively and dreadfully as a reminder of the price of revenge. The goblin descended upon them, doing so in such a way that all the light in the room was engulfed and swallowed up by its overwhelmingly large shadow.

At once, the twins looked at each other and knew. They nodded their heads in agreement and ran as courageously as their little legs would carry them to either side of the goblin. Being vulnerable, since it held the chair, the twins ambushed and captured each of the goblin's arms in their own. The goblin screeched as it felt itself being lifted off the ground. Its feet dangled in the air as the twins ran to throw that monster back through the mirror.

As they approached, the real Phoebe opened her arms wide to help ensure that the beast went through. The twins threw the goblin. Phoebe grabbed its arms, and with an almighty heave that required every single ounce of strength in her being, dragged the goblin through the mirror so that it went crashing and tumbling into the background with a spectacular thud.

In that moment, Phoebe remembered to jump back through the glass, and before she could even sigh a relief, she was back in her room, collapsing into the twins' arms. They embraced wholeheartedly, for they knew they were now safe.

The three of them looked at the mirror and saw the goblin boiling and convulsing with an ever-increasing and maddening rage. It bared its teeth at them, grimacing infernally. Together, the three sisters motioned that they would fall upon the goblin again, until it finally cowered and gave itself up to their threats. Very quickly, the goblin gathered itself and ran away behind the mirror, so that it now stood reflectionless.

Seeing this, Phoebe was troubled. Now that she needed the person in the reflection, she was not there. "Have I lost myself? Have I disappeared? Who am I?" she thought as she tried her best to collect herself. And as the time passed and normality seemed to return, so too did her reflection wander tenderly back into view as though it had just awoken from a deep and thoughtful sleep. At this, all seemed to be restored to its former and proper glory.

Phoebe knelt down and pulled both Natasha and Ioanna in close to her. All she could do was hold and squeeze them, and profusely apologize, through her sobs and hyperventilating. Yes, at one time she may have hated them, and even wanted them "dead," but not really. In reality, she did not want this at all, nor would she ever want this, nor would she even wish to act on such thoughts. It was feelings and emotions of the moment. But like all moments, these moments were transient, fleeting, and would undoubtedly and eventually pass, all the more so because she in fact really did love her sisters, despite how annoying they could sometimes be. And though this moment was cumbersome at the time, it could nevertheless still be reconciled, overcome, and in the end, moved beyond, and that was what Phoebe really wanted and desired most.

All the three sisters' faces glistened as the first rays of moonlight filled out the room. It was a befitting sign of the reconciliation that had just occurred and taken place between them, until the next great fight and struggle would indubitably arise to threaten and challenge them, as always seems to be the case with siblings. Alas, it was all in a day's work, and it was all the more sweeter because they were now together with each other again, after what felt like an eternity. They delighted and relished in the nectar of this bliss.

In due time, Ioanna declared, "we should smash and destroy that mirror."

Natasha nodded in agreement, adding, "so that this will never happen to us again."

Phoebe hesitated. "No, leave it," she said, holding them back with her hand.

"Why?" the twins asked together.

"Because" said Phoebe, "it will serve as a faithful reminder for us."

"Of what?"

"That we are what we make ourselves."

THE MAN WHO LIVED
IN DARKNESS

"You cannot go on seeing through things forever . . . If you see through everything, then everything is transparent . . . To 'see through' all things is the same as not to see."

—CS Lewis.

Once upon a time, there was a man who lived in a terrifying darkness. A darkness that seemed to be perpetual, relentless, and most harrowingly, without end. Now, this man was neither born like this, nor was he blind or affected by any other physical ailment or affliction. Instead, he suffered differently, in fact, he suffered rather unusually. Whereas any one of us could look up, see, and enjoy a flower, or a tree, or a butterfly, or the sun, for what it was, if this man was to do so, he would only shun and ignore them, or otherwise, see right through.

"Too bad," he would say of the flower, "it smells putrid," or "someone shall pluck it," or otherwise, "it shall soon certainly die." Or of the butterfly, "what a nuisance," or "why is it always in my way." Of the trees, he would say that they "take up too much room," and are "a waste of space," and of the sun, that it "always scorched," and was "too blinding."

Really everything seemed to be a problem for the man and otherwise, plainly, and simply just in his way. To him, it was all burdensome and bothersome, ugly, and insipid, and in this way his days passed, his darkness ever increasing and encroaching upon him.

So, as you can tell, his darkness was no ordinary darkness. It was a darkness of a very different kind. It was something learned, developed, nurtured, something akin to a germ or pathogen that had feasted and festered on the man for far too long until it had grown to such tremendous, cosmic proportions that he could not help but see darkness everywhere, in all places, all at once, even at the expense of everything else.

And for as long as Elizabeth could remember, her father had been this way, so much so that ever since her mother had passed, she slowly lost contact with him until soon, the chasm between them had become so vast that father and daughter no longer spoke at all.

To her father it was always this or that. "Do this, it's what I did," or "do that, because it's better than what you think," or "don't do this, because it's too much," or "don't do that, because it will ruin you."

She could never win, and after one too many of these constant barrages of "do it's" and "don't do it's," Elizabeth finally snapped. "Dad! You're *so* miserable. I can't take it anymore. Stop!"

And all her dad would reply was, "I'm just being real with you, that's life."

But it was not. Elizabeth knew this, but she could not express it in a way her father might understand, since he had so willingly obscured and secluded himself in his cave for far too long. All she could do was sigh in frustration because her father refused to see beyond his own way.

So, the years passed in silence, and her father missed all the most special and joyous occasions of her life, like the opening of her first business, her marriage, and even the birth of her first child, Anna. And though Elizabeth was plagued and riddled with guilt, it was not enough to outweigh her belief that her father would just say something to the effect of:

"Expenses on expenses on expenses that you can't afford, you'll ruin your life, and then you'll ruin yourself."

Elizabeth struggled with this and did her best to keep this hurt and pain at bay so that this darkness would not spread, pervade, envelop, and pervert her too. But every so often she cracked. The light was swallowed up, and the only thing that comforted her in those moments of tears was a silent prayer, that they might one day help to water the desert of her father's heart. When she had recovered, Elizabeth would remind herself of all the warmth, and light, and joy, and love in her life, and this encouraged her and gave her hope to go on. And on she went like a river, for everything inevitably flows.

By now, Anna had come into that age of curiosity where she could not help but question everything she saw and heard. One day, she was sitting in her mother's lap and a thought came to her like a honeybee. It buzzed around and she followed it with her eyes, twisting and turning her head to keep up with it until she watched it settle and nestle itself on her mother's shoulder. With all her youthful innocence and charm, she looked at her mother and smilingly asked:

"Do you have a dad, mum?"

"Pardon," her mother replied, totally caught off guard.

"Do you have a dad?"

Before Elizabeth could formulate what she thought might be an appropriate response, given that she did not know where this question had come from, Anna continued to bumble harmlessly:

"I have a dad, and I just wanted to know whether you had a dad, because I've never seen him."

"Yes, I have a dad," Elizabeth said, somewhat faltering.

"Where is he?" Anna asked, after a pause.

"Well . . . he's at his home."

Anna pondered thoughtfully for a moment before saying naturally, "I should very much like to meet him one day."

Elizabeth was taken aback. She began to soften and melt, adding "I'd very much like for that too."

"Then it's settled," Anna said very matter-of-factly, with that child-like honesty where it could not otherwise but be so, "we shall go visit, and see him at once."

In response, all Elizabeth could do was nod though she knew not whether it was in agreement or to satisfy Anna's fancy.

The next day, Elizabeth swallowed her pride and called her father against what she thought was her better judgement. She continued to remind herself over and over again that this was not about her, rather that she was doing this for Anna, and that seemed to strengthen her, and see her through. The phone let out a few rings and then she heard that same sure, stoic voice of her father, still unchanged, even after all these years.

"What do you want?"

"Hi dad, it's me."

"Elizabeth?"

"Yes, dad."

"What do you want?"

"Well, it's nice to hear your voice too, dad."

"Why should you care whether you hear my voice or not, you never call."

"I'm sorry dad, I've just been busy, you know how things can get."

"What does it matter? Soon enough I shall be dead anyways, and then I shall be no problem to you at all."

"What's wrong with you? Why do you always–" but she stopped herself. She took a deep breath and began again.

"We've had a child . . . "

"A child? In these conditions? Poor girl!"

"Yes dad, a little girl, Anna, and she'd very much like to come and meet you."

But her father seemed not to hear, let alone care, because he kept moaning about finances, and duty, and responsibility—all things he could not fathom Elizabeth could handle or take care of, perhaps because for so long, deep down, he knew he had neglected these things himself.

Elizabeth cut him off sharply.

"Look dad, spare me your lecture. I don't care. I'm not doing this for you, I'm doing this for her. She would like to come and see you."

Her father sighed pitifully.

"Promise me you will make an effort with her . . . unlike you did with me."

Her father groaned a groan that seemed to suggest that all of this was heavy, onerous, and exhausting.

"I don't care, and I don't want to hear it. Get it together, *for her*. Goodbye dad, we shall see you tomorrow."

And all Elizabeth heard was that sad and annoyed grumble as she put down the phone. She began to prepare herself for the battle she knew would undoubtedly come. Unbeknownst to her, Anna had seemingly floated in. She was studying her mother eagerly.

"Is everything alright?"

Elizabeth looked at her daughter and smiled a full, knowing smile. "Yes dear. Tomorrow we are going to see your grandfather."

"And your father."

Anna's words lingered in the air like a thick smoke, causing Elizabeth to choke and look away. Her mind did not know what to make of those words, what they meant to her anymore. She did not know what to feel, how to feel. Anna pressed her hand on hers. Elizabeth knelt down, hugged her, and spoke softly, sweetly, tenderly:

"Yes, and my father."

Without missing a beat, Anna embraced and squeezed her mother tightly. She refused to let go. She whispered in her ear:

"I'm so excited. I can't wait."

That night, Elizabeth was restless. She was plagued and torn asunder by "maybes", "what ifs," and "buts." Since she could not sleep, she went to check on her daughter. Anna slept peacefully. As Elizabeth stood in the doorway, she could hear the rhythmic beats of her breathing like the gentle pitter-patter of rain on a window or the easy ebb and flow of waves on the shore. These sounds comforted her, brought her peace, reminded her of all that was good, noble, and worthy in the world—that darkness was the necessary forerunner before the light. And because of this, she found the courage to stay afloat that evening to see the next day, a new day.

Anna woke up bright and early, dressed as smartly as she could, and scurried off to wake her mother so they could begin today's journey and adventure. She found her mother sitting up in her bed, gazing out listlessly. Though Elizabeth was reluctant and somewhat fearful, she could not help but be hurried on by her keen and ardent daughter who would ensure nothing deterred her or came in her way. If only it was always this easy to face one's dragons.

Soon after they left, they arrived at Elizabeth's father's house, and just like him, it was old, dilapidated, and neglected. Like a bad memory, some bygone remain, everything about it was tucked away, concealed, and otherwise repressed. It may have served as a mirror that reflected and reminded one of the quiet, hopeless desperation that the man's own life had now taken on and come to signify.

They parked the car and got out. They walked past the 'keep out' sign, through the dirt-plot garden, over the weed-ridden path to the cracked, peeling wooden front door. A sour, pungent odor, like that of expired milk, disease, or decay, filled the air. Anna could not believe that anyone would choose to live like this, for it seemed like one of those ancient and forgotten cemeteries that people force out of their minds and refuse to visit.

Elizabeth rang the doorbell, and together, the ladies waited. Nothing stirred.

"Is he home? Does he know we're coming?" Anna asked expectantly.

"He knows," her mother replied, "that's just him."

She rang the doorbell again. This time the ladies heard the growls and groans of a man that clearly was content and preferred his own idleness and apathy. They heard his heavy feet hit the ground, they heard the wheezes and moans as he pulled himself off the couch, they heard his muttering and complaints, "damn this . . . what do they want? . . . why can't people just leave me alone." They heard his pained trudging.

Finally, the door creaked open with that self-same heaviness they had just heard, and the two ladies stood before and were confronted by this hollow, shell of a man hunched over them. But what stared back troubled them immeasurably more, for the look in his eyes was beyond and far gone of bitterness and resentment, so that all that was left in them was a dim, empty, and apathetic dejection.

The man glared at them but said nothing.

"Dad!?" Elizabeth said in a voice that hesitated.

He let out a sigh and then turned his back on them to make way, saying:

"Well, you better get inside before people start asking questions, get the wrong idea, and complain."

The ladies moved hastily past, shook by the cold reception, though they did their best to hide it away.

"It's nice to see you Dad, you look–" Elizabeth began to say before she was cut off by her father.

"Just move on and go to the living room."

The ladies began to make their way, a way, but it was clearly the wrong way, for the man broke in again sharply:

"No, not there. It's across from you."

The ladies obeyed mechanically. Even at midday the living room was hardly "living." Instead, it displayed that ceaseless, fixed, and unchanging darkness the man had now chosen to live with and know. There was a single rocking chair, a single coffee table, on which was a single stereo, a single plate, a single knife and a single fork, and a single teacup. Not even Loneliness would have found a home here for the night, because the house was just big enough to hold and contain him. Everywhere reeked of his belief that no one was coming or would ever come for him again.

As they took it all in, Elizabeth struggled to find fitting, let alone any words to say. All she could do was fidget and fumble about, trying desperately, hopelessly to do anything that might lighten up the room.

Noticing, the man spoke sternly, "leave it. It's just fine how it is."

Elizabeth unwillingly shrunk and withdrew. She circled back and stood behind her daughter, resting her hands on her shoulders, perhaps for comfort, perhaps for protection, perhaps even for support. Finally, she managed to find enough courage to break the silence.

"Dad, this is Anna . . . your grand daughter."

Anna curtsied to the best of her abilities.

The man looked Anna up and down thoughtfully, and Anna in her turn, looked the man down and up curiously, both trying to better understand the other by getting as good of a look as they could. Though not a word passed between them, it would be better to say that it was like a meeting of two flames, one that had just been kindled and one that was on its way to being extinguished, for soon, the odd, and out of place pair strangely warmed up to each other.

"I'm parched," the man abruptly declared, out of the blue.

"And I'm famished," Anna added.

They both turned to Elizabeth as if trying to give her some cue. Then Anna asked sweetly, for the both of them:

"Would you make us some afternoon tea mum . . . please."

Though unsure, Elizabeth nodded and acquiesced. She disappeared into where she thought the kitchen would be, and though it seemed so strange to her, deep down she clung onto the hope that Anna and her father might hit it off and get along, even if it meant that it happened in her absence. She prayed and wished for Anna that there might be a relationship there with her father that she could not really remember having at all.

Back in the living room, Anna and the man continued to feel each other out in the silence. All that could be heard was a twitch here or a rustle there as they both tried to close the gap of generations.

"Pookie, stop it!" Anna suddenly burst out.

Whereas one might think the man would be dazed or confused, this was not the case. Rather, for the briefest of moments, a smile seemed to appear and escape from his lips, but as quickly as one may have glimpsed it, it disappeared, and he returned to being stony-faced and unfazed.

"Get away from there Pookie, leave him alone," Anna went on. "What's wrong with you girl?"

Anna ignored the man and continued her admonishments, this time with the stamp of her foot.

"You listen to me, this is not a game, come away from there, Pookie this instance!"

With those words, the man felt the breeze of what seemed to be a wisp run up his legs and back and settle on his neck and around his ears. It seemed that Anna had felt him out and knew him. Could she really know him? This thought took over the man, and like a pesky gnat, it buzzed about his mind biting, burdening, and bothering his otherwise calm and comfortable blackness. He tried to shoo this thought away, but to no avail because she refused to let up, to let go. How could this be?

"I can tell something is wrong," Anna said gently to the man, "I'll try and help you."

"There's nothing wrong girl."

But Anna seemed not to hear or otherwise she blatantly refused to acknowledge his interruption, for she was in the middle of conducting some very delicate surgery.

"Pookie, I shan't tell you again, get off his shoulders! Leave him alone!"

Immediately, the man could not help but tense his body and straighten his back so that he stood as strong and sturdy as a soldier at attention. He now stood upright with his chin and chest out, and his shoulders back, his hunch no longer apparent, and the shadow seemingly cast off, and out of him.

"That's better Pookie, be gone! This is no laughing matter," Anna said triumphantly.

The man breathed a bit easier, freer.

She softened and began to speak far more endearingly to the man.

"I'm sorry about that. I hope he didn't weigh you down too much."

84

"It's nothing," said the man stubbornly.

"It's okay," replied Anna, "I know that it must have been crushing you."

"I'm fine," the man replied bleakly, and he seemed to keep repeating these words if only to remind and prove it to himself.

Anna giggled. "It's alright," she said, "I know it can get heavy, but that doesn't mean you have to carry it alone, all the time."

The man wanted to erupt. "What would you know? You don't understand" but he stopped himself or rather, something else stopped him. He always looked down and perhaps he was by now so accustomed to doing so, that everywhere and everything he looked at demonstrated this. Now when he went to challenge her, he could not. He was mute, and felt himself floating, rising up, ever so slightly, even if it was very much against his will. For the first time in a very, very long time, the man looked up, and there in that gaze new hopes and dreams formed, for his gaze met Anna. She smiled a heartfelt smile which tickled him. Again, it had been such a long time since he had laughed and felt such warmth.

Anna held her grandfather's hand in hers, and squeezed it firmly, as though she would not let go.

"Things do get better," she said softly, "if only we look up."

The man looked at her. He had cracked, and so he pulled a funny face lest she should see a tear welling in his eye. By now, Anna could no longer keep it in and broke out into an uncontrollable giggle.

"What's going on? What did I miss?" asked Elizabeth as she just now had returned from the kitchen, carrying tea to these sweet, musical sounds. Here Anna was, like a seedling of light, sprouting and playing in the man's palpable darkness.

"Oh, nothing mum, grandpa was just being silly."

Elizabeth was not sure whether she had heard correctly, whether she could really believe her eyes and ears. She managed to stammer out:

"Well, it has been a long time since grandpa has been silly, so you better say thank you. You are a very lucky girl, Anna, I hope you know that."

Anna turned to her grandfather to say thank you for all their fun as exuberantly as she could.

The man bowed his head sincerely. He knelt down, pulled Anna in close, and whispered in her ear, very honestly, very seriously:

"No! Thank you!"

"Alright, should we eat?" Elizabeth eventually said, after their moment.

The man apologized sheepishly for only having stale biscuits and black tea, and for not having a more welcoming and hospitable spread. I suppose he had mistakenly come to think that that was all he needed to sustain himself. Nevertheless, it did not seem to bother the ladies too much for Elizabeth very quickly stopped him by saying:

"It's okay dad, were just happy to see you."

The man struggled but could not seem to bring himself to respond. It was all too much, too overwhelming, and now, he was uncomfortable in his revelation which caused him to become hardened and silent like before. And just as Elizabeth thought that perhaps something had changed with her father, she was brought back down, for the rest of their time was passed with shallow and hollow words or in awkward silence.

Not long after tea, the ladies left in the same strained manner as they had arrived. In the car on the way home, Anna cheerfully glowed though she did not say a word.

Finally, if only to fill the silence, Elizabeth said, "I'm sorry dear about today. I wanted it to be more. I hope it was not too disappointing for you."

"It wasn't."

"It's just . . . he's like that . . . that's him."

"I understand."

"Just don't take it personally. It's him, not you."

"It's alright mum, I'm glad we met each other. He's *my* grandfather . . ."

Again, silence descended swiftly like a thief in the night, robbing them of all their words. Nevertheless, Elizabeth tried again.

She was eager to know what her father said, what had transpired, and she could not help herself but ask Anna as naturally as she could:

"So anyways, what did he whisper to you, darling?"

"Thank you," Anna said simply.

"Thank you?" Elizabeth thought to herself confused. "What could he of all people be thankful for." Anna took notice of this in the mirror and tried to enlighten her mother, if only to make her see, to make her understand.

"Sometimes we all feel alone. And sometimes we just want someone to remind us that they're there."

"But–"

"We're never alone. We need only look up, look out, ask."

At home that night, Anna again slept peacefully in that way that can only come about after a good, long, hard day's work. But still, Elizabeth could not. She tossed and turned and wrestled with herself. "Was her father lonely, hurting, ashamed, afraid?" she thought. Whatever the case, she vouched that tomorrow she'd call him, talk to him, see how he is, how he *really* is, and try to be there for him like she remembered he had been when her mother was alive, when she was little.

Tomorrow would be the dawn of a new day for Elizabeth in her life.

Night came and went, and in the morning, while the ladies were breakfasting, the doorbell rang. Anna rushed to the door and was greeted by the postman who bore an unmarked letter. She thanked him, grabbed the envelope, and ran to her mother, repeating excitedly, "is it for me?"

Her mother looked at the envelope. It was faded with a yellow stain on the right-hand side. She did not know where it could have come from, so all she could say was, "let's read it and see."

She opened the letter and read aloud so that Anna could hear:

My dear, sweet, little, lovely Anna,

It was a pleasure to meet you. I sincerely apologize that it has taken this long.

I would like to invite you (and your mother) to tea. Properly this time. Please come. Please! I shall eagerly be expecting and awaiting you.

Love yours,

Pookie.

PS I know you, of all people, can appreciate just what that really means.

As she read those final words, tears flowed freely from Elizabeth's eyes like streams. "Pookie." That struck her in the depths of her heart, in the depths of her soul, at the very core of her being. In that moment, it all came back to her with a roaring crash. She remembered being with her mother. She remembered laughing, and dancing, and smiling, and picnicking together with her parents in the park. She remembered her father holding her hand while she chased butterflies and admired flowers and ducklings in the pond. Most of all, she remembered being picked up and cradled by him, all the while he caressed her and whispered tenderly, "I love you, Pookie, I love you, Pookie, I love you, Pookie." And now, here he was calling Anna "Pookie" too.

Elizabeth's reverie was broken, and she soared and surged back to reality because of Anna's begging.

"Can we go mum, please! Pretty please, can we go!"

It took Elizabeth a moment to collect herself. How could she resist the irresistible?

"Of course," she replied, not only full to the brim with happiness, but overflowing, "I'd very much like that too."

Anna cheered ecstatically. She was over the moon. And like a fairy that is given free rein in a field to frolic how it pleases, she began to rush about and press her mother.

"Come on mum, come on, what shall we write back?"

LILIES OF THE VALE

*"He who loves little, gives little. He who loves more,
gives more. And he who loves beyond measure, what
has he to give? He gives himself."*

—PORPHYRIOS OF KAVSOKALYVIA.

"DRAW LOVE."

"Huh."

"DRAW LOVE!" exclaimed Whisper, even more forcefully
than before.

Can you even draw love? Now that is a *real* question. Perhaps
for someone like you, this is not an especially serious question, a
question that can easily be dispelled or done away with, and that is
understandable, fair enough. But this is not the case for me.

For me, this is the type of question that belongs in that cat-
egory of questions that we might call, "life changing questions,"
questions like: where do thoughts and dreams come from? Why
does the sun rise? Where do flowers get their fragrance from? How
many times do you have to kill a dragon before it actually dies? Do
princesses fall in love with ordinary people? What happens in the
ever after? And most of all, who am I? You know, these kinds of
questions that take hold of your mind like an octopus and squeeze
it so tightly, with all its tentacles, so that it is almost on the verge of

suffocation, demanding not only an acknowledgement, but also an explanation and an answer. Yes, those kinds of questions.

And so, accepting this octopus, I set out on an adventure to try to find an answer to this question: how does one draw Love?

As I sat in front of my page my mind wandered as it tried to conjure up images of Love. I scribbled a big, bright red love heart—but that was not it. It was far too obvious, too childish, too boring. But then another image stole me away and I quickly and furiously tried to catch and imprint it on my page.

I saw my mother and father, my siblings, the beach at twilight, ice cream. Especially ice cream. Strawberry to be precise. In a cone. Right at that point where it starts to melt, spill, and dribble down your fingers as thick and sticky as honey, and it becomes a race between you and that ice cream to see who, in that moment, will accomplish their goal first.

I had it. Voilà! Love!

I showed my siblings. They trilled and giggled with delight—obviously of course, how could they not. So, then I went and showed my parents. Now, they seemed proud of me too. They could not help but show off my drawing, proclaiming boldly and enthusiastically, "how charming and splendid it was," and that they "might have an artist on their hands," as they stuck the drawing onto the fridge for everyone to see and admire.

That litany of voices still follows me, haunting me by repeating over and over again just how lovely and beautiful my drawing is. But something is off. It does not feel right. For underneath that echo, a subtle but nevertheless certain, nagging voice persists. A nagging that undercuts and slashes through this seemingly hollow, empty humbug. A nagging that no one else seems to hear, and if they do hear it, sure bear, hide, and conceal it better than I ever could.

"Your parents, your siblings, the beach at twilight, ice cream— these things aren't Love," says Whisper, "they're things *you* love."

I am baffled. What is Love?

Whisper continues to repeat himself, more and more insistently. "Draw Love. Draw Love. Draw Love."

"Why?" I cannot help but ask out loud.

"Because," answers Whisper, "everybody knows that Love is the beginning and end of all things."

So now, again, I find myself in my original predicament. But then something else hits me, in fact more than that, crashes onto me, like a ton of bricks. I think I know; I think I understand. I cannot help but smile stupidly, since I have been made to look like a fool. I have made a spectacular oversight, have had a complete and total lapse in judgement, forgotten one of the most important things. How could I not know what Love is? I quickly scribble her sketch onto a new page, and behold, I have it. My first 'real' Love.

"That's not Love. That's Iliana."

Oh Iliana. That terrible, terrible Iliana. Everybody remembers *her*, their first Love, how could they not? But what can one say about them, that enigma? With her cascading chestnut hair, her wide and kind chestnut eyes, her caterpillar-like, chestnut eyebrows, and her violin string lashes, she was like a sweet, Spring symphony for all the senses to behold, savor, and indulge in. Or in other words, a music to your ears, a music to your heart.

But more than this, she was another one of the cosmos' rare gifts. Iliana, like all young ladies, was at once both a priceless treasure, and her being, the corresponding map that was waiting ever so patiently to be deciphered and understood so that all her secret and hidden riches might be brought to light and gleam. And when all of a sudden a first Love strikes, this mystery opens up to us and attracts us, like the vastness of the ocean, exerting its pull so strongly and in such a way that one cannot help but give themselves up to it and be swept away from the safety and steadiness of the shore, ever deeper into its swell.

Given that Iliana was all this, perhaps I could be forgiven for thinking she really was Love.

That day, I waited for her in the garden amongst my precious flowers, that spread and etched their colors out before me like a magnificent painting, and in the shade of the great oak tree, that served as the frame to contain it all, filled and consumed with all my hopes, dreams, and fancies. Perhaps, this very well may have been my own Eden. Iliana was coming to visit, and I tried as best as I could to occupy myself until that moment when she would fatefully arrive.

"What could she be doing? What would it be like if she was here right now?" I allowed myself to wonder, getting more and more lost in the lingering myrrh, and myrtle smelling fragrance of longing and anticipation.

I heard a faint but nonetheless familiar sound, like the humming of a beehive. Imagine if that was Iliana. What would she be laughing and chatting about? I was enchanted by the melody of those mellifluous sounds and could envision her smiling too. If only I could know what she was thinking, feeling, whether she concerned herself in any way with me.

A gentle breeze picked up and began to caress and tickle me. I could feel it ever so lightly dance and graze over my skin, and I imagined Iliana's hair wavering before me, wistfully, wonderfully. If only I could be the wind to touch her, to be near her, to plant a kiss on her warm cheek, as the wind does a flower. Oh, how much would that all mean.

A shadow began to creep up and I thought I could make out her likeness and features in it. I could envisage her walking, nay floating down the way with her dress ever so slightly bobbing. What charm, what grace. If only we could be together. But the shadow cawed and grew wings, and before long flew away. Perhaps it had only come to tease and tantalize me.

A twig snapped. Could that be her? It must be. But what should I do? Iliana echoed inside of me, and my heart uttered things my lips dared not say aloud. All I could think was, "I wish she was here, right now, in this garden next to me," as though I was casting some spell.

"Peter."

I burst out laughing for such was my creative power it seemed. Not only could I imagine Iliana, but I could even converse and play-act with her too as if she really was here before me.

But that soft, sweet, sure voice called out again.

I turned to look, and there she stood, scintillating sacredly and splendidly, in all her glory, like the most elegant and beautiful of all flowers, underneath the gaze of the almighty sun. Oh, what a vision, a vision that had merged and mingled with Nature, with Earth, with Life itself, in such a way that each could not help but complement, enhance, and ever-beautify the other. This must have been what the great poets spoke of when they closed their eyes and imagined.

"Iliana? Hi," I managed to stammer out, still in disbelief.

She smiled bewitchingly. "Who else could it be?"

"You are real right? You are you?" I asked, wanting to confirm because I still was not so sure, "this isn't a dream?"

"How can I prove that?"

"Kiss me," I said, half-jokingly.

"No way," Iliana replied, through a giggle.

I nodded my head in satisfaction. It was worth a try, for things like that only really seemed to happen in dreams.

"Kiss you . . ." Iliana repeated before trailing off, still chuckling, and playfully hitting me on the arm, "that would be–"

But she did not finish her thought. I think she could feel my gaze on her cheek. She turned to face me and soon we stood there in silence, lost in each other's eyes. Even if it were only for an instant, how does one recover from such a stare? Luckily, I did not have to, for she whisked me away by hand to go and explore my flowers which she had just noticed.

"Wow, they're . . . they're . . . beautiful," Iliana was compelled to declare in her rapture, trying to take and breathe in each intricate, extraordinary, and individually created and stitched flower, all the while I fascinated over her.

And right at that moment, I found an opportunity to take charge, to take over, to show off, and flaunt my flowers, if only to increase her joy, increase my joy.

"You see these ones," I said gallantly, pointing to the lavender, "do you know why they're colored purple?"

"No, why?"

"It's because when fairies fly past, the buds tickle their wings and feet causing them to sneeze fairy dust which in turn makes them turn purple."

"Really, then why have I never seen it happen before."

"Ahh," I answered jestingly, "it's because it happens at night, and you're not used to seeing such things."

"I am so," retorted Iliana, not to be outdone.

"I don't think so, and even if you could see like me, I doubt you would believe."

Iliana smirked at this silliness and light-hearted fun. "Well, what about those ones professor," she said sarcastically, now pointing to the daisies, "how did they come to be?"

"Mmm, the superb and exquisite daisies," I said, making a show of it, "they say that unicorn hairs are knitted together and woven around different colored jewels so that when the moonlight shines on them, it forges them together so they cannot be torn asunder, and it brings out their many different and hidden colors and charms."

We both erupted into an uncontrollable laughter, a laughter that could last a lifetime, that could echo until eternity, a laughter that must have been something akin to the feeling of the many winged seraphs and cherubs bubbling around in the hallowed halls and palaces of Heaven.

Iliana continued her journey, closely and thoughtfully inspecting each of the different flowers, while I quickly snuck off to find the biggest and most delectable pearly-white lily to give to her.

Having found the one, I snapped its stem as easily as one might snap a twig or a neck, and I thought I heard a soft yet painful whimper. But I could not be sure, because I was too caught up in my ecstasy to take notice, let alone care. After all, lilies do not hurt and cry, do they?

I quickly returned lest I spoil the surprise, with the lily out of sight, behind my back. I tapped Iliana on the shoulder, breaking her reverie, and she turned. I blushed and my smile continued to grow, largely against my will, perhaps even giving away far more than I had intended to.

"What?" she said enchantingly.

"I have something for you."

"What is it?"

"It's a surprise," I said, uncovering and revealing the flower.

Iliana stared but did not so much as even utter a sound.

"This is for you," I managed to tremble out as pleasingly and playfully as I could, "it's a lily for Ili–ana."

Iliana merely stood there and examined the flower, but her expression remained blank and bare as if she was undecided or worse, as if she did not care and felt nothing at all. She let out a sigh.

"It's because I really l–" I let slip, if only to fill the silence, and quell the doubt the was beginning to fill my mind.

"I like roses, they're more beautiful. I want a rose."

"I'm sorry," I managed to stammer out timidly, almost mechanically, not knowing what else to say, all the while I choked back a tear. I hid my face to recollect myself and when I looked back up, Iliana was gone. She had almost danced her way down the driveway, disappearing out of sight like a snowflake lost in the snow. She dropped the lily, and I felt its thud as it hit the ground, deep inside my heart.

The garden became a lonely place, lonelier still now that Iliana had gone. She was yesterday's flower and all I could ask myself was, "is that it? Is that all?"

"Why did you do that?"

"Not now Whisper," said I, grief-stricken, "I don't care to hear it."

"Why sir?" that voice called out again, in a way that might have even rivalled the fall of Man.

I would have strangled Whisper if I could have, but the more I tried to suppress and stifle him, the more I realized it was not him talking. In fact, he had not spoken at all.

"Whose there?" I called out into that abyss.

Tiny voices began to ululate, almost to the point of a howl. "Why did you do that?" they kept crying out over and over again, as if in a cruel, nightmarish performance.

"Do what? What did I do?"

The wailing died out. Then a single, solemn voice spoke, full of pain. "Why did you cut off her head? Why did you sacrifice her to that girl?"

"Cut off her head? Sacrifice her? What are you talking about?" Had I heard correct?

The voice quickly became fed up. "You will look at me when I talk to you. For too long we have been quiet. Now we demand to be heard."

The words made me dizzy and sick as if they were like clubs bludgeoning my head, raining down blow after blow. I fell to my knees. Behold, I was face to face with the lilies.

"Good. That's better," said a lily milder because she had softened, "I will ask you again, why did you cut off her head and sacrifice her?"

I had no answer. The lily could clearly see this and continued:

"You see that flower was not yours to take, nor was it yours to give."

"But what's so wrong?" said Whisper, supposedly coming to my aid, "this is a flower after all, it has no life. Who is it to speak to you like this? Is not the flower yours, to do with it as you please?"

The lily sensed and felt deeply this wickedness and pitiful defence. It addressed me, now speaking slowly, strongly, sharply, pronouncing and emphasizing each word of its judgement as if it was a whip.

"Hear me and hear me well. We are not your slaves, nor are we playthings for you to do with us what you please. We are lilies. Lilies to be loved and enjoyed."

The words lacerated and cut. I was speechless, guilty, what defence could I make?

Immediately, the lily whistled a whistle that seemed to call the garden to life, as if it was calling me to enter into, and glimpse a fantastical and perhaps even forbidden new and secret kingdom. In response, a finch answered its call and perched itself by the lily's side.

"My old friend," said the finch, "it's been a long time. What can I do for you? What can I help you with?"

Without saying a word, all the lilies looked at me, convicting me with their eyes, and then they bowed their heads in a mournful silence that got heavier and heavier the more it went on and was endured. The finch immediately understood.

"*How* could you let this happen? *Why* did you let this happen?" said the finch, turning to face me.

What could I say? I tried to mutter something, anything in response, but ashamed, I could not even bring myself to speak out.

"Where is it now?"

"It's lying somewhere along the way," I said, stuttering in return.

The finch flew away obligingly, and I was left all alone, for the lilies seemed to ignore and forsake me. Then the shame, the guilt, the reality began to sink in. It had been so long out of the soil, away from water, torn from its very essence, from its very being, and left on the cold cement to wilt away. Surely it was dead. It must be. And worse still, I had killed it. I began to panic and shake. What Hell was this?

"Don't beat yourself up," said a lily, seeing me wither. Somehow, it still had the heart to want to come to my side, comfort, and alleviate my anguish and suffering, despite its own. "It just means you must learn to love bigger, love better, love more."

"But if only I knew . . . if only someone told me . . . I wouldn't have done what I did . . ."

"I'm not so sure. Even if someone told you, would you have listened? Or would you have done what you willed to do still anyways?"

"It's not my fault. No one ever said anything. No one ever told me."

"Or perhaps they did. Except you just never really heard, you just never really listened."

I was on the verge of retaliating and unleashing a tirade if only to vindicate myself, but the lily humbled me.

"That's not the point. It doesn't matter now, dear boy, what's done is done . . ."

But I did not want to, nay I refused to acknowledge that, to accept it, to believe it, so much so that I was too caught up to hear the lily utter its hope.

". . . that's life—up, down, life, death, death, resurrection—so now we must look back up towards the light."

By now, the finch had returned, and I could see it carrying the lifeless lily in its beak.

"Is it dead?" I cried out miserably, "have I killed it?"

"Have you any faith," said the finch, after placing the lily ever so gently and tenderly on the ground.

"Faith? What has faith got to do with anything?" I said shrugging my shoulders, "is it dead or not?"

"I guess we shall have to see," the finch answered curiously. "Dig a hole in the soil," it now commanded.

I instinctively obeyed. I knelt down and began to remove the soil to create in the patch of dirt a hole deep enough to lay the lily down in. It was the least I could do for this poor darling. Having done so, and filled with compunction at my act, I could not help but ask, "shall I bury it?"

"Is it dead?"

"What kind of question is that? Is it dead? Why of course, it *must* be dead. I killed it with my own hands. I can see it for myself," I said, although my words faltered and became more and more hesitant, unsure, and uncertain the more I went on. A doubt or a hope began to creep in, though I could not be sure which. How could I truly know?

"Plant the lily," said the finch with an all-embracing and sublime serenity, "it lives, or at least it shall live."

"But how? How can you be so sure? What if it really is dead?"

"Ah my boy, though it may seem beyond you, it is true. Even the dead live, they live by Love."

In silence, I planted the lily in the plot I had dug as lovingly and as tenderly as I could. I covered its resting place in soil and found myself weeping over it, beyond my will. Perhaps they were tears of sadness and sorrow, perhaps they were tears of hope and joy for what might come. Whatever the case, they watered the earth, endowing and baptizing it with new meaning, with new life, as I watched on praying and waiting for some miracle to occur.

"Rest well now, my friend, rest free," said the finch and the lilies together.

"What happens now?"

But neither did the lilies or the finch reply. Instead, the bird flew away, and the flowers assumed their same stoic impassivity as we are usually accustomed to. And I was left to wander alone, aimlessly around my garden.

I noticed a weed overgrowing near where I had just planted the lily. Not wanting it to defile or corrupt the flower's growth, I knelt down, dug my fingers into the dirt and ripped it out by its roots. As I looked up again, I caught sight of a whole infestation of weeds and thistles that I had seemingly neglected, that were now attacking my beloved and precious flowers.

How dare they try to spoil and ruin my peace and joy, I thought to myself. So, I set about weeding, pruning, and otherwise purifying my garden beds, all the while sighing gently and whispering kind and caring words to these beautiful living creatures. Whether or not they heard me or appreciated my work, I did not know, but I could not care, because really, I was more than happy to quietly sacrifice myself for them, my newfound friends.

Before long, the hours had passed, and the sun was beginning to set. With new eyes, I took the garden all in, and now it shone, radiated, and gleamed resplendently, having clothed itself with glowing white garments of light.

I was exhausted and worn out, yet I was overflowing with thankfulness and felicity. I had forgotten all about Iliana, or rather, I had seemed to let her go and move on.

"She's yours, you know," said Whisper, all of a sudden, assailing me.

"No she's not."

"Do you not love her anymore?" asked Whisper temptingly, "are you done with her already?"

"No," said I, as I thought about my flowers, about all that had happened to me, "I love my lilies."

"Good, that's what I thought," said Whisper, "so grab her, take hold of her, make her yours, never let her go."

"But—"

"She's *yours!*" exclaimed Whisper harshly, "isn't that what you said?"

"No! I love my lilies. Not only that, but I also love all my flowers. In fact, I have come to love and will continue to grow in my love for all those things that find a home in my garden."

"Your lilies, your flowers, your garden, yes, you are so close," said Whisper enticingly, "you are right there, right on the cusp. Just take her! Take, and steal what's yours."

"No!" I cried out triumphantly, "I just want my lilies to be."

For how could it be possible to share in something precious, or even begin to embrace your love, if your hands are otherwise so tightly clenched?

Whisper was silenced as quickly and as suddenly as a tempest, or a raging sea might be quelled when they obey the command to be still. I stood there smiling, freed, completely, and utterly moved by this new way of living and being. You could not even begin to know or understand how proud I was of my heart, of that victory.

"Might this be Love?" I asked myself, as I breathed it all in.

"Draw Love. Draw Love. Draw Love."

"Yes," I thought, "I need to capture this. I must capture all of this. But how?"

"From above," now purred Whisper, lullingly, "for only from there can you see and perceive all things clearly."

Something about Whisper's words strangely affected me, something about their grandness. If only I could touch the sky and see the world from above the clouds, down below, then maybe, just maybe, I might be able to make sense of it all. Oh, to be a little giant, how easy would it all then be?

I laid eyes on the great oak tree which stretched its branches out over the flowers and high up into the sky like a loving king might, who seeks to watch over and protect his people. Though it rose immensely above them, it seemed to remind, inspire, and call them up, so that they too might rise up steadily to his splendid heights, if only to meet and greet him there. After all, one can only imagine just how much the oak tree had seen.

I hurried up its trunk and nestled myself on a branch in view of all the flowers, especially my lilies. I began to obsess over every single one of their details, trying to capture each unique crown and curve so that my drawing might kindle and electrify.

"Draw Love. Draw Love. Draw Love."

But how? I had not the tools.

Something stirred in my very depths, from the place where something even before knowledge and understanding make their home. My heart panged, and so too did the garden pang with the most ancient of pangs. It was as if the flowers, and the birds, and the trees were within me, beat within me, and I within them, as if something else, something more, was enriching us and giving us life. We were in total harmony, euphoric union, as if we were all truly One.

A bird perched itself next to me on the branch, if only to rest for a moment. I reached out my hand to pet it. It did not flinch but stayed calm, grateful for my soft touch on its head. It turned and left a feather on the branch, winking knowingly at me, before flying away and melting into a cloud. I picked up the feather and held it to my heart.

There was a splinter, then a creak, and then a crack behind me. I instinctively turned around and saw a piece of bark, the exact size of a page, drifting down and somersaulting in the breeze. I reached out to grab it. I pulled the paper into me and treasured the rich, glossy brown wood that was unlike anything I had ever known before.

With my feather and bark, I had the necessary tools in my hands, and I began to scratch out onto my page Love. But with that ear-piercing screech, something was still off, something was not right, something was still missing.

Ink. That precious blood, that precious seed by which I could touch and expand myself into the ether. As I paused to ponder this, I dropped my hand beside me, but instead of falling, it was stopped, as if it was being held up by some invisible force. I felt a splash on my fingers. I turned to look, and a single lily had risen from below the earth, above all the others, all the way up to the branch where I now sat. My hand was in its pearly-white crown as it offered up and blessed me with its particular and peculiar ink. I dipped the tip of the feather into its crown, and the ink stuck in what was one magical fusion.

"Draw Love. Draw Love. Draw Love."

I looked out to the horizon, the last of the sun was poking over it before it would inevitably disappear for the evening. I thought I could make out my lilies of the vale, twinkling as early night-time stars, but something shone even steadier and brighter behind them, beyond them, outside of them, as if it was this light that was igniting and sustaining them all. I smiled, as this light glowed on me, in me, through me.

You see, the bird gave me its feather, the great oak tree gave me its bark, the lily gave me its ink, and I truly felt and experienced all these wonderful and magnificent things.

"Draw Love. Draw Love. Draw Love."

The words kept repeating inside of me, taking over me, replacing the blood flow in my veins, the air in my lungs, even replacing the very beat of my heart.

I looked up to the sky, and with newfound strength and spirit, I gave myself up and poured my heart of hearts, and soul of souls, and mind of minds onto the page vividly, the beginning of an endless work, and it was good.

Ah, so this is Love!

A FINAL WORD BEFORE
WE FINISH . . .

IT IS FINISHED, OR better yet, it is accomplished. What is, you might ask? This. This collection of short stories, this voyage and celebration of words, this constellation and mosaic of Love. Yet I cannot help but feel that this is not the end, but rather only just a beginning.

What I have tried to flesh out and bring to light is that intimately individual and yet uniquely universal feeling and experience of Love. Of the aromatic fragrance of your most favorite food that your mother or father cooks for you each week for family dinner; or of picnicking in a park with your friends, laughing, smiling, living, and dancing, with not a care or concern in the world, existing for the moment, grateful and affirming all that is; or of feeling all the care and tenderness in the world of that person, *your person*, who brings you a glass of water right before bed, reads you a story, hugs, and tucks you in, kisses you on the forehead, and wishes you all the best so that you might sleep well and dream even better.

In other words, I have sought to express the 'lightness' of waking up in the morning, each and every day, bursting forth with joy and brimming with thankfulness for a new and fresh start, wanting to share, over and over again, all our dreams, and warmth, and happiness, and love, with the people we love.

If this is only a beginning, it is precisely because, as the great saints, mystics, poets, storytellers, artists, and fools of the past tell us, and attest to, I have only been able to reveal and bring forth a flickering flame, *my* flickering flame, of the wildfire, or my delicate droplet in the ocean, or my single shimmering shooting star in the galaxy of what we call Love—a 'little' love against the backdrop of the vastness, expansiveness, and ultimate greatness of the 'big' Love. And that is alright, that is okay.

I must recognise the sheer enormity, and impossibility of such an endeavor, of my own insufficiency, and inadequacy. It would be remiss, and beyond me to think I could capture and hold all of this in the palm of my hands, for it would be like trying to clasp at sand all the while it slips and falls through my fingers. So instead, I can only satisfy myself by passing *this* on, by pointing to this grand and incomprehensible, though not fictitious, or unknowable mystery, and hope and pray that I have encouraged you enough to dive, headfirst, into it for yourself so that you might come to know it better and more fully and provide its missing piece.

For me, what these 'little' loves—whether they be the flowers, trees, landscapes, creatures, kids, Nature itself—seek to illuminate, offer, and show is a certain disposition, a state, a particular way of being. We should become like gardeners, like dancers, like poets, better still, like children, imbued and enriched with sensitivity, simplicity, gracefulness, humility, and especially an overwhelming and unwavering *willingness to love and be loved*, so that we might be able to discern and acquire a harmony, unity, and oneness with ourselves, others, and the world around us, despite how terrifying, challenging, and vulnerable that means we may be. That way, not only might we come to a keener, clearer, and more anchored understanding of this 'big' Love, but more importantly, actively share and partake in its mystery and glory if only to be able to then soar among the stars, in the currents of infinity, in the palaces of eternity, in that which is most good and beneficial for us all—or to put it another way, to dwell in paradise.

In the absence of this, "Hell," Dostoevsky writes is, "the suffering of being unable to love." For me, this is because when we content ourselves by saying that the knowledge of Love is superior and higher than Love itself, we lose, ignore, and ultimately miss out on Love's wisdom and experience. Theories, ideas, or abstract principles, when it comes to Love, to Living and Being itself, are no more than puffs of smoke, phantoms, will-o'-the-wisps—artificial, fleeting, illusory, and ephemeral. Instead, we should aspire and work towards Love's sensation, towards its praxis, towards its experience, towards the opening of our hearts to its warm and gentle embrace.

If there is a justification and answer to suffering, it is beyond explanations, beyond words, it transcends all these things. It is born and comes out of action and direct engagement and experience with Love, so that in spite of all the angst, anguish, sorrow, misfortune, misery, hurt, and pain in this world, when we toil, cultivate, and water this—*our Love*—we can declare, alongside Dostoevsky, with deep reverence and gratitude, in earnest, and with the most intense triumph, "I exist. In thousands of agonies—I exist . . . and there is a whole life in that . . . "

I could not have said it any better myself.

To sacrifice, to make effort, to burn for Love, that is everything! Because surely there is nothing more ineffably perfect or sublime than to have something built on Love, nurtured, and sustained with Love, multiplied by Love, that is to say, to have Love unobstructed, Love uninhibited, Life everlasting and Love never-ending.

Alas, perhaps here lies the door to the beginning of all the wisdom that places the onus and responsibility wholly and squarely on us, a wisdom that boldly, beautifully, and poetically proclaims that the Kingdom of Heaven is within each and every one of us all. May we continue to live out this mystery, and struggle and persevere ever fearlessly, faithfully, courageously, vigilantly, and patiently upwards towards these heights, even if it is only by way of start with these meagre sillies, fancies, and trifles.

PK 2023

THE END
FOR THOSE CHERISHED
FEW.